MY L
SEARCH FOR LOVE

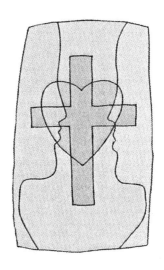

(A RESTORATION TO ORDER)

GRACE M. JONES

Copyright © 2003 by Grace M. Jones

My Desperate Search for Love
by Grace M. Jones

Printed in the United States of America

Library of Congress Control Number: 2003100857
ISBN 1-591604-21-4

All rights reserved. No part of this publication may be reproduced or transmitted in any form or by any means without written permission of the publisher.

Unless otherwise indicated, Bible quotations are taken from the Holy Bible, King James Version. Copyright © 1966 by The National Publishing Company. Printed, bound and published in the U. S. by the National Bible Press, Ph, PA

Xulon Press
www.XulonPress.com

Xulon Press books are available in bookstores everywhere, and on the Web at www.XulonPress.com.

CONTENTS

Acknowledgements .... *vii*

Dedication .... *ix*

INTRODUCTION .... *xiii*

GOD IS LOVE *17*

PURPOSE *19*

WHAT THIS BOOK IS NOT *23*

EXPLANATION OF WRITING ORDER *25*

MY STORY *27*

HOW WE MET *29*

MY REAL VIEW OF MY MAN *49*

I WANTED TO BE YOUR LOVER, NOT YOUR MOTHER *53*

HOW DID THIS HAPPEN? *55*

HOW DID I GET THIS WAY? *61*

REASONS THIS HAPPENED *65*

I AM GOING TO MAKE HIM LOVE ME! 67

WHAT MY EXPERIENCE TAUGHT ME 69

THE BREAKING POINT 73

*GOD WANTS TO GIVE YOU HIS BEST,
     WON'T YOU LET HIM?* 75

THE "KEPT" MAN 77

*WHEN HELPING SOMEONE IS REALLY
     HURTING THEM* 81

SMELLING THE "COFFEE" 85

YOUR EMOTIONAL FALLOUT 87

HIT BY A TON OF BRICKS! 89

WHY DIDN'T I SEE THIS COMING? 91

EMERGENCY RESCUE "911" 95

*THE TRUTH OF THE WHOLE MATTER AND THE
     BOTTOM LINE!* 101

BURY THE PAST AND MOVE FORWARD 105

VALENTINE'S DAY 109

THE "GREATEST NEWS" YOU WILL EVER HEAR! 111

TO RECEIVE THIS GREAT GIFT FOR YOU 115

*SCRIPTURAL PROOF OF HOW GOD FEELS ABOUT YOU
     (King James Version of the Bible)* 119

ACKNOWLEDGEMENTS

A SPECIAL DEDICATION TO MY GIRLS

To my Girlfriends that have helped me throughout my life and have listened, given advice, and been with me through the good times and the bad. They have also endured the **DRAMA,** while I was going through it, I Love You All and Thank You for being there for me.

Special Honorary Thanks to **Cylinder Thomas and Sheena Currington Miller,** who lived this experience with me, who consoled, encouraged, understood, and lovingly guided me through this ordeal Thank God for Girlfriends!!

Debbie Harper	Paula Barry
Cassandra Barry	Donna Cole Beasley
Ronika Jones	Helena Plat
Paula Pleasant	Honey V. Butler
Monica Ball	Michelle Brown
Binita Miles	Shirley Hayes
Mary Griffin	Jackie Farrington
Cheryl Allen	Linda Lestage'
Bettye Sanders	Jackie Walker
Debra Kelly	Margaret Brown
Lois Tyson	Linda Colbert

Special Thanks to Chris Agard, who made this book possible and encouraged me to follow my dream!

DEDICATION

To God, Who is very much alive and real today. God, the Creator and initiator of "REAL LOVE." GOD IS LOVE!

To all of the relationships that I've experienced that brought me to this point in my life, good and bad, they have all played a major part in shaping and forming me into the woman I am today.

To my parents, may God rests their souls, Tommie and Flossie Jones, who loved each other for Thirty-Three (33) years until my father's untimely death. It was my father who showed me a "Godlike Love," being the first image of love by demonstrating it through care, concern and a provider for me.

My Desperate Search For Love

Flossie Mae Jones

Dedication

To all of my 16 Brothers and Sisters, I love each one of you so much. Thanks to all of you for your love and I am honored and abundantly blessed to be a part of such a special group of people. We have endured many good and bad times, heartaches and pain as a family, but you all made it worthwhile and you are all my greatest treasures in life.

Marilyn Jones Anderson (Deceased)
Edward Jones (War Veteran)
Doris Jones Washington
Michael Jones
Shelia Jones
Shirley Jones
Norma Jones
Stephen Jones

Carolyn Jones Scott
Marine Jones Larks
Alexis Jones Elder
Tommie Jones, Jr.
Debra Jones
Clarice Jones
Kathy Jones

**Ronald Lewis Jones (Deceased in infancy) Dearly Beloved

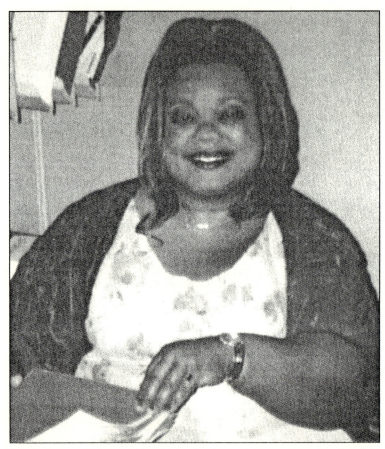

Grace M. Jones

INTRODUCTION

*M*y soul is soo vexed over all of these television "Judge Shows" (and you know the ones I am talking about), showing beautiful intelligent and well-to-do women who are bringing law suits against men that they have given thousands of dollars, jewelry, furniture, clothing, rent-free living accommodations, or aid with their rent, bought them cars and literally became "Sugar Momas" for these men.

Now here you are on "Judge Whoever's Show," trying to get what you have given back. It is so sad!!!

What angers me more is that these men have the nerve to say, "Your Honor, it was a gift, She was just a sucker waiting to be licked." Now here is the sad and tragic reality, WE ARE GUILTY AS CHARGED.

Of course, we didn't just give without expecting something in return and we did it because we loved and cared, but regardless of the reason, we end up getting played because a man should take care of himself.

Women we must learn that we cannot buy our men. Oh sure, you can give him all of the above-mentioned things and guess what, he will gladly receive them from us, but we are looking for something in return and then when we don't get it, we get angry, hurt and want to sue or take some other drastic action, because we feel like we've been robbed.

We as women hope to buy love and affection and some of us are so needy and hungry for some male attention, we don't care about money, things or whatever we have to give to get attention and affection from the opposite sex.

Understand me, it is not my intention to dog out the Brothers, and I am speaking only of the ones who prey on women, you know who you are, but my intention is to show you how to avoid becoming a victim and getting played.

The horror of the reality is that we put our ownself in this position out of genuine love and concern, where we are looking for LOVE, and they are looking to get LAYED AND PAID.

I was a bonified Member of this Club, but I am proud to say that I am an Ex-Member. I am not belittling my sisters or my brothers, because I was a serious "SUGAR MOMA" and because I loved my man so much, I felt that it was my duty to take care of him.

I began to take a poignant look at what caused me to react the way I did and through my story I hope to enlighten and make others aware of my plight.

I discovered that many of us have been raised without a Father present in the home or if he was in the home, we never formed a Father-Daughter closeness. To be loved by a man who truly cares for us, to protect us and look out for our total wellbeing, simply because we are his daughter and because he loves us, is something awesome to have and experience and if we did not have this, we have a void and a hunger for it and we will stop at nothing to fill this void.

I feel this was my case, but I also know women with solid relationships with their Fathers that simply desire to be with a man so bad they will stop at nothing. I am not an authority, but I only know what happened to me.

I once heard a sermon and this preacher had five daughters and loved them all. He said that the FIRST man who ever holds you gently and kisses you tenderly with pure love should be the first man that sees you and that man should be your Father on the day you were born when they placed you in his arms in the delivery room!!

This is so precious and so true, but sadly many of us missed this and many of us never had a Father around to teach us what we should look for in seeking a male companion and a life-long mate.

God has the greatest compassion and pity on us, because He

knows that we do not know any better and I mean that literally. You can't do better if you don't know better.

Many of us women are so hungry and lonely, we carry a label on us and it reads I AM DESPARATE.

It is just like having a giant name tag on and then you wonder how everyone knows your name! It is that obvious to those who can read us like a book and pick up the signals we are unknowingly sending.

God is offering you "REAL LOVE," Unconditional Love, true and deep. The kind of love you don't have to try to earn or try and purchase by giving material things like money.

God's love is there for the taking, just because GOD IS LOVE and since the beginning of time, He has already made up His mind to love you just for who you are.

Love is a choice and God made it His choice to love you.

Love that comes because you perform favors or give material things IS NOT LOVE! It is so sad that even after my experience of giving everything I had to win this man's love, He still did not love me. I found myself broke in my heart and in my wallet, and yet I still came up empty and I felt robbed, swindled and violated.

If your love, marriage or relationships are based on these previously mentioned terms, what will happen when you can't give any more or do any favors any more? Does that mean that the love is gone? If it does, guess what, IT WAS NEVER THERE.!

God wants to show you exactly how to get the true love, the real love that your soul has been hungering and thirsting for and I hope through the pages of this book you will discover the meaning of TRUE LOVE.

So get ready to enter my world and take this enlightening journey of my experience and share in my newly gained wisdom and apply it to your own life and don't take it lightly because this book cost so much to write and it is the second most precious gift to you, the first and even more precious and valuable is God's gift to you, which is HIS LOVE.

GOD IS LOVE

*S*ince God is Love, the measuring stick begins and ends with Him. Only He can help us determine what is real love and what is not, because no one knows you better than God.

We all need love, from our cradle to our graves and with God's divine guidance, we will be better equipped to make better decisions concerning love and stop making these terrible and fatal relationship choices that always end in disaster.

It is time to put an end to this painful process and let's seek God's advice so that He can help end this dreadful cycle.

If we keep doing the same things we have always done, we will continue to repeat the same painful process and ending up with the same results.

Hopefully with advice from my experience and God's help, we can change the equation and end up with positive results.

PURPOSE

My purpose in writing this book is to share with you my plight as a woman who encountered nothing but pain, deceit, mental and emotional abuse, devastation and heartache that was caused by me.

The saddest thing is to reveal to you is that these things happened to me because of what I allowed someone to do to me, due to a low self-esteem and poor self-image and not loving myself enough to stop it. Remember, no one can make a fool out of you unless you let them.

I was so eager to be loved that I allowed myself to give money, time, mental and emotional care to men who only cared about receiving these material favors, who did not care about me. The worst thing in the world is to be in love ALL BY YOURSELF.

I began to write about my experiences in the hopes that I can help some other sisters and women in general to avoid this painful wake-up lesson. If you read this book and learn from what I went through, maybe you won't have to go through it.

My book is also being written because I know that I am not the only one who is going through this.

Many women are involved in relationships where they are the ones who are doing all of the giving and meeting all of the provisions, such as paying the rent/mortgage, paying his bills, whatever it takes to meet a man's needs to keep him and make him happy.

Many of us keep this kind of thing under wraps and hope that nobody knows just how low we have stooped. I know because I sure did not want my family and close girlfriends to know. What woman wants to look like a fool? We worry about what will my Mother, Sisters and family think of me, if they knew that I give all of my money to him, allow him to drive my car, allow him to live with me rent free? What will they think of me?

The real and true scenario of this question should be, "What do you think of yourself?

The very reason you hide these facts is because you are ashamed. Yes, ashamed, because I bet all they are providing for you, as my man did was sex.

Some women are content with that, but I am not. I want more than just a bed partner, because if that's all he can do for me, what do I have when he gets out of bed?

When we finish sexing all night long, bills will still need to be paid and life goes on outside the bedroom.

My purpose is to help other captives go free.

Women of all races, saved, unsaved, rich or poor, no matter your height, weight, size, shape—all walks of life.

Women, we are all a specially made creation that God took His time in creating with an awesome purpose in mind.

We are as a delicate flower; we are made from man, for man to be a helpmeet and partner for man.

We are also the very glue that holds our families and marriages together. We have been divinely endowed by God with a "power" to make or break our men.

Beginning at birth, we have such a profound and powerful impact on our baby boys, being able to carry them in our wombs, then to suckle them at our breasts and this forms a deep and impacting bond, virtually unbreakable. We become everything to them and we try to use this influence to nurture, guide and counsel them into manhood.

Women are strong, powerful backbones. We can be as fierce as a lion, or as gentle as a lamb.

There is nothing in all of creation like a woman and that is the way God intended for it to be.

In this so-called "New Day" and new millenium, we are in extreme danger.

We are not the same women as our Mothers. We even consider some of their ways to be so called "Old Fashioned" and out of date and calling it that old time stuff, but they certainly were doing something right, because they kept their families clean, fed and together and we would do well to examine some of these "Old Fashioned Ways" for some of the answers for today.

Our Mothers did the best they could for their day, my Mother, Flossie Mae Jones, birthed 17 children, loved her husband, kept a clean house, did laundry, cooked home-cooked meals everyday and kept her family together. She was an exceptional woman!

We all can't be like my Mom, but we must restore ourselves back to our "Original Queenship." We must fight tooth and nail to regain our thrones our homes, our men and our babies and re-establish our place of influence given to us by God.

We are the backbone and we need to take control of ourselves and stop acting like weak, desperate, wimpy brainless women, who can't think for themselves because we lose all sense of reason chasing after these men.

I am not pointing finger at you alone, because I was guilty of this very thing, but we need to "Get A Grip," "Put Ourselves In Check," because we have ruined our men by giving them everything and then we turn around and ask them "Why don't you stand up and be a man?," Let's face it, YOU ARE NOW THE MAN!

Our men need our help to be "Men" again, but we must take a united stand to demand that they treat us like the women we are and treat us right and respect us for who we are.

We must put this thing back to its proper perspective and restore order before it is too late, and with God's help we can do it.

Until we re-claim our Queenship, we cannot help our men to re-claim their Kingship. We must do all we can to restore our men back to a place of pride, dignity and manhood, because God's greatest creation, in my opinion, was the creation of "MAN."

WHAT THIS BOOK IS NOT

*T*his book is not a male bashing book, nor is it an attack on women, rather it is my story of my dilemma of blindness and how God helped me to get my sight back and how he freed me from an unhealthy relationship and showed me my symptoms and patterns of behavior that will help me stay free.

For the men who are hardworking, responsible husbands, fathers and heads of households, or single men who are just trying to make an honest living and provide for themselves, I HONOR AND RESPECT you!!

Thank God your kind of man is still out there!! So often, we tend to focus on only the THUGS, SCRUBS, BUMS, LOOSERS and the decent hardworking brother has a tendency to always get overlooked.

If you are a man who falls in this category, this book is not about you.

Women, if you are a woman who is self-sufficient, self-supporting, strong, independent, who loves herself and never let a man mistreat you, I APPLAUD YOU ALSO, and this book is not about you either.

This disclaimer is necessary so that my book will not be misunderstood, because it is not intended to hurt anyone, but to be used as a guide of what can happen when you allow yourself to become so lost in another, that you stop loving yourself first and put another person's needs, wants and desires before your own for the sake of love.

The real tragedy is when you give yourself wholeheartedly and *love so deeply, only to find your are in love all by yourself. That is when the hurt and devastation begins, YOU ARE IN LOVE, BUT THEY ARE NOT!*

EXPLANATION OF WRITING ORDER

My style is a little unconventional, but I will share with you my eye-opening experience first and then I will attempt to show you my life from my childhood and some of what I consider to be contributory factors that led to my dilemma.

This does not mean that this is how everybody will end up that starts out like me, but I think we all have similar occurrences that leave us yearning and hungry for someone to love us.

Your story may not be like mine, your life could have always been filled with love and maybe you never had a deep sense of yearning, but you still ended up being the man in your relationship wanting the wrong man to love you and taking care of him.

All I am trying to say is that anyone of us can because of love, fall into this same situation. We have all been a fool for a man at one time or another and many of us wish we could have seen some things coming before we got played, taken advantage of, been hurt, or used by someone who we cared for, but the feeling was not mutual.

So the order of this story is first, how I ended up and what made me see the light, then a brief review of my life to see how this yearning and hunger snowballed to cause this situation. O.K., Here we go . . . . . .

MY STORY

(MY DESPERATE SEARCH FOR REAL LOVE)

THE AWAKENING

*I*t is 4 AM, I can no longer sleep. I am hurting so hard deep within my soul. I feel like the character in the Bible named Jonah, I am in the belly of the whale.

I am trying to sort out my feelings. I feel like I could kick myself.

My financial needs . . . . Oh, God, my financial needs are so great for all of my unwise spending, I and I alone am left with the responsibility of getting out of all of this debt, self-induced and self-inflicted debt.

I am literally robbing Peter to pay Paul—I am trying to decide just how many days I can eat before I get paid again. I don't need food every day, right?

My rent is now two months past due and I am on the brink of eviction and the same is true of my car note. Let's not even talk about regular utilities!

I am praying that none of my relatives try to come and visit me because I don't know what utilities will still be on and if they do come, I don't have any money to feed them. Please Lord, don't let anyone visit me now.

I have $1.00 in my checking account and my savings account is officially zeroed out.

In the midst of my despair, I say "God Is Still Good!"

How did I get in this predicament you say?

I am embarrassed and ashamed to say that I am a victim by my own hand.

No one told me to give all of my money little by little to my man, but that's what I did and now look at me!

This situation did not happen over night. First, I found myself so blinded by wanting the love of a man so bad that I allowed myself to be so consumed in him, that I put my needs wants and desires behind his.

I didn't realize that I didn't love myself, until I began going above and beyond financially, mentally, emotionally and sexually for this man.

I loved him so much that I didn't want him to want or hurt for anything, but the tragedy is they took, took, and took and acted like I was making all of the decisions for him to take, but he offered nothing in return.

I was not only coming up short with my man financially, but I was also being played romantically. He never offered any type of genuine care and concern for me in ways of kindness, gentleness and tenderness.

He claimed he had trouble expressing emotions.

What have I gotten myself into?

HOW WE MET

Beauty Is Only Skin Deep

I was attending night school when I met this young man trying to further my career and he just happened to work there as an all around maintenance man. I was transcribing a tape at a computer with a headset on my head and my first mistake was to take that first look.

I looked up and all at once the heavens opened up and I saw the entire universe and entire galaxy! I had to compose myself and in my mind and heart, I said, My, My, Oh, My!!!

I realize now that you can't go by how someone looks, but sisters, this man was so fine, I would later discover that he was a former model and it wasn't hard to believe. I knew someone like him would definitely not be interested in me, as fine as he was. Get real.

My heart leaped within me and I got butterflies whenever he came into view. I was at a real dry spell in my life, no one to love and no one to love me back. I am a hopeless romantic and my heart began to have fantasies of what if he and I could be friends, then lovers and on and on and on!

My priority was in the wrong place and I went for what appealed to my eyes my heart. We women don't think of all this practical stuff when we see a fine man, we just look. When a man is so fine, how can we think rationally? Please don't let him look good, smell good and then flash a smile at us, Hello! I Surrender! Game Over!

I think that all of us women have a weakness for a handsome man with a muscular physique and they are pleasing to the eye, but when you have experienced being in a relationship with one of these "Pretty Boy Adonis's" and they take you for everything you have, you grow up fast!

I know that you are suppose to keep your senses about you and use the good sense that God gave you and hold on to reason, but when you are lonely and have been for some time, you don't think rationally and what looks good, ain't always good for you!

I began to discover that this fine specimen of a man was single.

Let this be a clue to you, whenever a fine man is by himself, something is up!

So every night when I arrived at school early I would see him, so needless to say, I would make it a point to get there in time to see him. My heart would race and my heart would increase in palpitations whenever I saw him.

We began to speak and hold conversations, with each one becoming longer than the previous one.

My heart would say, Could this be? Something must be wrong with him, can't he see I am a plus-size sister and most men don't like me because I am not a size 6, wonder what is up with this, but Hey, I am going with this for as long as it lasts.

This man sparked a place in me that had been dead for so long, just the excitement and anticipation made me feel so beautiful, and womanly, I don't care where this thing is going, but let's keep the hope alive, you never know. Even if it is nothing else but a friendly thing, it is better than the nothing and the invisibleness that I am so use to. Men overlook me, no matter how pretty my face is, how beautiful my hair is, atleast he is paying me some attention and I have been so hungry for that!

I didn't want to be too forward so I would simply be cordial and then my last day of school, he asked me for my phone number, so I gave it to him.

Now every relationship that ends up in disaster didn't start out like that.

I began talking to him on the phone for hours on end and we seemed to have some things in common, but I found out that he had to serve time in jail on the weekends for ticket violations and he was serving his last weekend when I met him. So here I am, on the phone with him in jail all night and he wanted to spend the time with me on the phone so it would pass quicker and at the end of this time, he wanted me to pick him up so I did. He asked if I was hungry and took me to breakfast.

In my mind, I said I don't want any jailbird, but the fact that he was working and at least offered to buy me breakfast and his being fine, made me believe I can handle this.

Another determining factor to go ahead with him was, unfortunately there were no other men interested in me at the time. Believe me when I say that my Black Book was not full of suitors, Please, I don't even own one and my phone was not ringing off the hook.

One of my girlfriends and I had a phone conversation and we came to the conclusion that we women must feel a inner spark, butterflies, tingling in our toes, or some sort of ignited light within us that goes off that cues us to know, Ohhhh Weee, I sure do love him. A feeling that makes you know you are alive from the dead and this is how he made me feel and I knew this thing just felt right.

During breakfast, I would learn more horrifying news. He was the father of Seven (7) children and he was married to none of the mothers, and led me to believe he was paying child support, I would later find out that he didn't. His story just kept getting worse and worse, but it was still not enough to run me away, not because of how fine he was anymore, but because he seemed to have so much Drama in his life and I felt I could help his life having some counseling and missionary experience years earlier.

I know a lot of men are down on their luck and need a break, so I felt sorry for him. I found out he still lived at home with his mother and he took me by to meet her. We then picked up his VCR and went to my house to watch movies. We picked up dinner first and I paid because he had paid for breakfast, but let me know that the money he had was his last. So I knew he was broke.

We ate our dinner and watched the movies and I felt so wonderful just to have a man who wanted to be with me again, I just overlooked all of the negative things I learned about him and just wanted to have a good time.

My heart went out to him and I began to feel that I could help his life.

I told him that I never sleep with a man on the first date and then drove him back home to his Mother's.

So on our second date, we went to the movies and then we visited one of my girlfriends, who had invited us over for dinner. Well, you know how we are ladies, we think we have such a fine man, we want to show him off to our girls. So after dinner, we drove home, it was so dark and he knew the way better than I, so I let him drive back and he was suppose to drive himself home, but took a detour to my house. I told him this was not in the plans, but he remembered in his mind that this was our second date and he wanted to have sex. Well, I can't lie, it had been a long minute for me too and I could not bear any longer just to keep sitting around him making small talk.

My friend at the time, did not beat around the bush, he walked right in and made himself comfortable, totally disrobing and felt comfortable in the nude and I was not use to this kind of wild man, but it I ain't gonna lie to you, (bad English, I know), but I acted embarrassed but I loved looking at his body. I had never seen a man more buff and toned and never had one been in my home and wanting to be with me sexually.

While with him, I forgot all about rules, regulations, values, principles, morals whatever. I was caught up by him and swept away and this only increased to a greater level after we slept together. I felt really good when I was with him and he made me feel good. I was happy and began to make plans for making a future with him.

I had no idea of what I was really dealing with. I immediately noticed that after we made love, he would get up and go in the living room and smoke a cigarette and then he would want to watch television all night long and constantly raid my refrigerator all through the night.

This behavior really didn't disturb me at first, but I began to feel that there was an emotional problem, as we made love, it really turned out to just getting some sex.

This man did not treat me like a cherished jewel and hold me and *touch me tenderly afterwards, he would just get up and do his own thing like a routine. I then began to ask him back into the room and he began to make up all kinds of excuses like the mattresses were to hard and he preferred sleeping on the couch and I really didn't recognize that these signs were indicative of other issues he had.*

Sex was not the only thing that caused me to begin to love him more and more. He could not express his emotions, but he began doing things that men do for me, maybe I should have acted like it was nothing, but no man ever did these simple things for me, like taking out my garbage, fixing things, cleaning up the kitchen for me, a lot of things in the place of giving me money or taking me places.

My boyfriend was never ashamed to take me around all of his family and friends. As a matter of fact, he would show me off and be proud to hold my hand in public and never ashamed to give me a little Sugar in public or to put his arms around me at any time. These things meant a lot to me and I felt good, safe and secure with him around me.

My boyfriend's life was so filled with turmoil, the more he got in my soul and I began to get deeper and deeper into him, the more horror I would learn about him.

He explained to me some childhood abuse that caused him to be so cold, (You have to be careful here, it could be true but sometimes men who only want what you can give and don't want to share any emotions with you frequently use this one—It is not that they can't show any emotions, they simply refuse to.)

On the other hand, there are some legitimate abusive cases and it could seriously affect a man, you just have to know if he is telling the truth or not.

My boyfriend's life was so full of turmoil and disappointments that I felt it was my personal duty to help him out and rescue him. I felt nobody understood him better than I and plus, I was lonely and had this need in me to help him and to try to make him happy.

I felt that it was my personal missionary rescue to save him. So I began taking a very careful and analytical look at his life and trying to apply a Band-Aid to a huge gash wound.

His problems began to be bigger and bigger and even more drama was revealed to me. Again, I was determined to help and make a difference so nothing scared me away so far.

I learned the full extent of his driving record that was full of warrants for his arrest that he simply neglected to pay and that he was driving without license and insurance. I really got scared at this point that this man was not even afraid of the law and his mother had given him a truck to drive and he acted just like he was legal. He began to get into trouble and involved in running from the police so he would not get caught and do more jail time.

The next thing that scared me was that he worked a job, but was always broke wanting more money and always wanted me to pick him up at the same location all the time. I would later find out that he was giving blood plasma to get even more money. (What in the heck is up with this man, I thought, He really needs me.)

His problems became too big for me to help him with and it seemed like the more I did for him, the more he would want me to do. I had previously gotten to the point that I told him that I loved him in an effort to help heal his life and at the time, I really felt I did, but he did not love me, but used my words to prey on my emotions to get what he wanted and he would tell me "I thought you said you loved me" to try and get things out of me. This began to show me he didn't feel a thing for me, but wanted to use the statement only to get me to act in his behalf.

Instead of reading the signs for what they were, I still felt that God could help him, so I tried to start taking him to church. This didn't help.

God can help anyone, no matter how impossible the situation, but they must first desire to be helped, such was not the case here. He acted liked he was being entertained, he felt good, but he didn't feel the change, he did not respond to the alter call, because he felt the pastor was talking to other people, not him.

Things got even worse. He began to stop working altogether!!

I would later discover that the job he had when I met him, had fired and re-hired him three previous times. So this was a pattern with him.

Once he called me from his mother's house laughing and making jokes about being fired the fourth time, because he claimed he was in the hospital from a police beating and he simply failed to *call in. He then decided to stay home and watch cartoons instead of getting out and looking for a new job. It was as if he was relieved he got fired.*

All of these actions were indicative of a deeper problem. This was more than a case of laziness. It was more serious than that!

He then began to stay at home everyday and watch cartoons and collect his unemployment check. I then began to realize just how he fathered all his children, constantly laying in bed all day long and then trying to have sex with me unprotected, because he liked how it felt. I always refused and made sure I was armed with protection all the time. He always wanted to have sex and never carried any protection. So he loved to take chances promising me he could pull out in time. I don't think so, and girls don't fall for that or nine months later you'll know why.

This became a regular routine for him, living at home with his mother at the age of 43 in her unfinished basement and did not offer to pay any rent, nor help with groceries or any other bills and yet his favorite line was that the "White man" was holding him back. Please!

I felt sorry for him and began to realize that this was more intense that a person having a bad break in life—that this young man really needed some serious help. I stayed in his business constantly.

I started helping him to find another job. I sat him down and got all of his necessary details and typed it up, called and set up appointments, giving him money for gas, cigarettes and tried to meet all of his other needs, always hoping that he was just experiencing a dry spell or a lull in his life and that this would pass.

I started going back to church and I believed that if I showed him enough kindness and good deeds where he could feel the love of God, maybe he too would come to the Lord. I was able to get him to come to church with me and he acted like he was at a concert or show, not moved at all. I was so stupid and blinded that I felt he would come around eventually, he just needed a little time. He never attended church again, and it influenced me not to go as often so I could be with him.

So here I was into a man with no job, no love for me or God, no goals, drive or ambition, only keeping me sexually active, no real emotion or tenderness, well, I guess we might have well been DOGS, the act was so cold and routine, no one should be subjected to this kind of abuse, talk about coming up empty!

I took all I could take; I fell to my knees and began to ask God to help him because I knew He was the only one who could. God answered my prayer.

Job offers began popping up everywhere, but somehow he would never get the job, it was always someone else. So he continued to act so depressed and wanted to stay at my apartment- not because he wanted to be with me, but that was what he wanted me to believe, but so he could watch my cable and relax all day.

I know what you are saying to yourself, "Girl, what did you get yourself into?"

I began to ask myself the same question and said, "What kind of man did I get mixed up with?"

He would asked me if he could stay at my place while I went to work.

His request was too ridiculous for me to grant. I had previously declared that I would never let a man stay in my house and sleep in my bed while I had to get up and got to work, but there is another area where I allowed my standards sink to an all time low, and I allowed it.

That day when I left for work, I felt like my inner soul died within me. I could not believe that I was really letting this happen and that I allowed him to break me down like this. All day at work I was sick as a dog. I played into what he was working toward all along. I was so mad and angry with myself, because my car and my little apartment were all I had.

I had visions of him falling asleep while smoking and burning my apartment down, Oh, you just don't know how I agonized.

I know a lot of sisters are saying, boy she sure was stupid, but when you get hung up and deep into another person accepting anything just to make the other person happy, compromising your beliefs, this is how you end up!

God let me know that I am not the only one who is like this.

Upon my arrival to my home, I was so mad with myself for letting this happen, I would come in and find him still sleep in the bed.

I would look at him with such hatred for making a fool out of me by allowing this to happen, I had to look back in retrospect and realize that I played a major part in him not standing up as a man, because I was doing everything for him, and I had assumed the dominant role, he couldn't be the man because I would not let him! I was a major accomplice in helping him not to be the man he could be. I HAD BECOME THE MAN!

We can't demand men to become men, while we offer them crutches and excuses in the form of what we call help. Our "HELPING" is really hurting and crippling.

A "Real Man" will take the help you give and then help himself up. I am not vindicating that we don't need to help men who are genuinely in need a helping hand and will pay us back later, but the problem is, you should not put yourself in this position, because you may not get your money back.

If a good, decent, sincere man is genuinely down and needs help, God will show you, but just try not to get in this situation, because so many people are running scams and are hurting people behind this in the name of love.

Feeling that my boyfriend's problem was that he just didn't like the kind of work he was doing, (still not willing to give up on him) I began asking him, just what did he love to do and tried to help him search out his dreams, desires and visions to see what he would be happiest doing.

I discovered that he had several friends with muscular injuries and back problems, of which he helped to massage them back to health. I felt, within me, there it is, Bingo! Now we have discovered his talent!

I know you are thinking at this point, Hasn't this girl learned her lesson yet? When is she going to quit? Well, the answer is no. I hadn't learned my lesson, I still believed his situation was not his fault. He was a victim. So I made up my mind to help him once again.

So excited that we have finally tapped into what was really going to help him, I borrowed $300 from a local cash leasing program in order to send him to a school for massage therapy.

I was so proud of him, I went with him for his enrollment and orientation. I paid for everything, wrote checks to cover his expenses including his books, the total sum of $500. He was a perfect actor and he had me fooled as he pretended to be excited and promised to pay me back every penny. I was so happy to do this to help his life and I finally put his life on track, boy did I feel good about this!

I made an awful mistake, because I gave so much and made it easy for him, since it did not cost him anything and all he had to do was show up, It didn't mean anything to him. Unless you pay and suffer for something yourself, you'll never know how hard it was to achieve and you won't appreciate it.

It is just a part of human nature, when things come easy to you; you don't have an appreciation for what you haven't worked hard for.

My efforts were very short lived. He had agreed to attend school during the day session and then work in the evenings. After only four days in school, a great job offer came up and when they could not reach him, they contacted me. Ecstatic and happy, I called the school to inform him concerning the job, only to find that he was not in school.

Puzzled, I thought he went home and I called there and his mother said she hadn't seen him either and that the persons wanting to hire him called her also, so we both assumed he was at the interview.

Later that evening I was in anticipation of hearing good news and he came by and I asked him how was his interview. He replied that they had given the job to another guy, who just happened to be white.

I had heard this story so many times, that I felt whoever this one white man was, I wished he would stop following my man and getting all his jobs! I even told him that this made me mad. Please don't let anyone use this lie on you because it gets old and played out! He kept getting knocked out of job after job and I suspected something else was going on.

I really saw his true colors due to this behavior and the horror of what I was really dealing with.

My man was not the Victim, I was! Victimized by my own stupidity and blindness to see him for the Con Artist and Perpetrator that he was! He really played me and treated me like I was naive and stupid. He was running a game on me the whole time. Everytime, he was called for an interview, he would decline.

He did not want to work or to go to school either. He wanted me to take care of him, because I told him I loved him, he felt that because he was providing me sex, that I would do anything for him, including taking care of him. He had no intentions of working, nor of paying me back any of the monies I had previously invested in him, nor to carry his own weight and take a load off me. (I had created this monster, I am sad to say).

My gut instincts kicked in during this time and he received a call for another interview, I knew about this one and asked him after the interview of the outcome, still he did not get the job. So he needed to make a run and left my apartment, while he was gone I called the employer who wanted to hire him and he told me that my boyfriend called and canceled the interview stating that he had a family emergency.

When this manager told me this, my heart fell to the ground as if it weighed a ton! Can you imagine the hurt and pain I felt to discover that he was such a liar and when I asked him about the job he made up a big fantastic story about how it happened.

I don't want to sound evil or hateful, just enlightened to what was really going on. I should have taken a hint from a previous time. I had mailed his picture to a prestigious modeling agency and they wanted to use him for wedding fashions and bridal shows and he looked to me to pay for everything, but I could not afford it.

So we sought out another opportunity with me again mailing off photos to a reputable calendar publication and they selected him for a slot as Mr. September. He was required to take one shot for one photo shoot and receive $500. It was legit. I went with him for the interview and heard all of the conditions. It was set, we had the date and time for the photo shoot and when that day arrived I could not find him. His mother had not heard from him, he would not answer his cell phone and he would not call me for three days. The company asked me to desperately try and locate him, but after three days, they used another model to take his place.

I knew that it was either drugs or another woman or maybe that he just shut down due to the drugs and he was hiding out somewhere.

He called me after a week and I let him have it, but it was him, not me. I was pissed at how he could just throw money-making opportunities away and he wanted to do little jobs like mowing lawns, or hauling garbage, but only whenever he felt like working.

I was so livid and disgusted, I can't make him work if he is going to lie and cancel his own job interviews. This was deeper than I realized. I really began to get scared, Help me to help him God.

I can't believe it, but once more a door opened at a prestigious company we had faxed his resume to. The job called me and told me all of the information and details and I prayed that this time he would follow through. Thank God this time, he did.

He was so cute to me because I saw how badly he really wanted it this time was different. He was so scared and nervous he brought all of the documents and paper work to my house so we could carefully do everything together and so it would be right. He wanted my opinion about what to say about every question and he was really scared.

The day of his interview, he was scared to death and had to report that morning at 7am. He was so scared that he had to come by my house first and let me see how he was dressed and re-check his paper work, Lord I prayed please bless him with this job.

I know he was scared it was an all day, in-depth interview with drills and exercises and role-playing drills. It was to last eight-hours.

When he showed up at my door, I knew it was really for me to hold him in my arms and to tell him with assurance that I believe in you baby, you can do this and if it wasn't for you, you would have been disqualified before now and I saw him that morning turn from a boy to a man and leap down my stairs and rush down the highway with confidence that me and God had his back.

Later that evening he came by to take me to dinner because he had passed every test with flying colors and he had received a photo I.D. with the name of the new company and he said I have you and God to thank for this!

So we enjoyed a night of fun, excitement and relief and hope for the future, his future and I thought our future together and I felt I was vindicated for staying by his side and that all former things provided or done to make this moment possible was worth it all!

He began working and even having overtime.

He was hired as a temporary at first then made permanent. It was with a very well established fortune 500 corporation and for once he began to take on responsibilities. He began to pay his fines, tickets, and other bills.

I was so happy for him that I did not jump down his back for all of my money that he owed me. I was so glad that he was out of my pocket by buying his own beer, cigarettes, gas and anything else he needed. He also started to call me when he got of in the morning (he worked from 7pm to 7am) and offered to take me to breakfast. I could not believe it. Finally, I actually saw a total change in him and I saw his life change because now he felt more like a man.

His behavior was so different, it was like he had a purpose to be. Everything he did surrounded his job.

When I saw how hard he was working and how excited it made him to have money again, I felt good. He also began getting more and more landscaping jobs on the weekends. So now he worked 12 hour shifts and he even began working on his off days.

I was happy for him, but I began to miss him more and more. I began to feel that he was avoiding me. He was now running from me because he had money and wanted to do what he wanted with it. I began to tell him that he needed to pay his fines and secure his driver's license and renew his auto insurance because now he had the funds to do it. He avoided me and he also did not want to give me any money or to pay me back.

I told him to handle his business so he would never have to go to jail again. I also found out he was missing jobs because he had not way to be contacted, so I had an account with a local cell phone agency, so I helped get him a cell-phone since he was doing so well and now had a job to pay the bill.

So here was my boyfriend, finally working, paying his bills and had a cell phone. I could have not been prouder. Sometimes he would come over with new tennis shoes and running suites he had bought for himself. You should have seen the pride in him. I had enough pride for the both of us. He also got where he would give me money to and buy groceries so we could have dinner that I would fix.

I was so happy for him. I would begin to see less and less of him and he would not answer his phone at times. So I would wait until he called me.

One day out of the blue, he came by my house as if he was being chased by the police and I could tell that he was not himself. He told me that the day before he did not go to work. I said well we all need a day off at some time, no big deal. He said, no Grace, I didn't call in or go in, which we know in any sense of the word means FIRED. I asked him why and he said because he ran from the police and was afraid that if he went to work they would follow him there.

First of all, he did not get his license and insurance as I had asked him to do so he would not have to run from the police any more, but he wanted to do whatever he wanted with his money and began hanging out with his friends drinking and I had asked him not to do that, because he always got in trouble. His moods and actions started being so erratic at times, that I suspected some Crack use as well and I do not play that Crack mess.

So he lied to the job and told them he did not show up because he was in jail and had received a ticket. He then asked me to forge an old ticket he had at his house to help him to keep his job.

I was shocked and appalled.!

Of course, I said no, because there was no need to lie or falsify documents for you doing the very thing I told you not to do and don't try to pull me in it now that you have messed up.

I knew he was going to get fired now and that it would be only a matter of time, because the job asked for the ticket. They never asked for it.

He would be working for a total of four months now and then he received the news that one of his baby's mothers would file papers for garnishment of his wages for child support, which would not have happened if he started it on his own as I told him, since she was a newborn baby. He was also behind on support for an older child.

Once these things began to happen, the company made further investigations into his file and background and found out other criminal convictions that were not told to them and for neglecting to inform them of this information he was fired.

When this happened I was so hurt, but I also believe that he lied about something else he did, probably not showing up again, only

God knows.

I only know I had had enough now. I was really through this time!

I had exhausted all of my energies, strengths and efforts on this man and unless he was willing to help himself, there was nothing no one, me or God, could do for him. I later confronted him and told him that I was stepping out of his life, I was so exhausted, I could no longer deal with his life and irrational behavior and could no longer deal with this situation.

I tried everything in my power to help my man's life, but you can't do it all by yourself. I am glad for at least a little time of seeing him become successful, but he had not changed other bad habits that led to his firing and I saw no end of this continuous pattern and it had been 6 years from the time we met to now.

I felt like I had no blood in my veins and I felt his failure was mine too.

I had to realize that I had gone above and beyond the call of duty to help this man and it makes me angry to hear some brothers say that women won't deal with them unless they have a bankroll, a Mercedes or Lexis, not all of us are like that, but the few of us trying to help men that are down, we get played and come out on the losing end.

This young man was now 44 years old and the only definite thing I knew he was sure of wanting to do was lay around in bed all day and watch cartoons and eat ice cream, while I would get up and go to work and take care of him. He felt that he was providing me with sex and that should be pay enough in return!

It <u>ain't</u> enough sex in the world for you to lower, belittle, and degrade me!

He felt that his sexual favors were his ticket to a carefree lifestyle, while I go out and earn a living for the both of us, NOT SO!

I can get mad if I want to because I have a right because I suffered, but guess what? The blame is still on me though, because I helped to create this monster and I brought it on myself, but I was not going to take this any more, nor was I going to add to this mistake by continuing in my mess, once I saw the truth.

I will take the responsibility of being wrong by providing and giving to my man and I will admit to being a FOOL for thinking I could by his love and I will admit to being a FOOL in believing that I could change him, but I refuse to keep on being a FOOL, now that I have seen the light. Nobody is going to keep me in bondage, even if it is a form of bondage that I created for myself.

I told my boyfriend, my man or whatever I thought he was, to get out of my apartment because I could not stand another minute of his mess, I simply could not take it any more, my nerves got bad and I didn't even care about his being fine, please! When you get to this point, everything you thought you felt has been killed out of you so, you don't even want that man around you, you are literally sick to your stomach and the things that they have done to you—make them just as ugly as the ugliest monster you ever saw!

No one has to tell you when it is time for your breakthrough moment, your girlfriends, family and loved ones can try to talk to you, but when you know it is over and you have had enough, no one has to say a word, you know it in your very heart and soul. It is like a yoke on an oxen's neck and you feel just like Atlas trying to hold the weight of the world on your shoulder and all your soul cries out for at this point is relief and you do whatever you have to do to get it and get FREE!

I told my boyfriend, since you don't have a job anymore, that cell-phone is still in my name and on my account and I don't want my credit messed up so bring me the phone so I can turn it in. Well, he says, Grace, don't you think that that should be my decision? I said, I'll give you two weeks to get another job, if you don't, bring the phone to me so I can turn it in!

He did not get another job, nor did he bring the phone to me, so I had the company cut the phone off. I was then charged a $400 fee for terminating the contract early, but I didn't even care, I took it as a loss along with all of the other monies and all of the other pain, suffering and hurt I invested into this relationship—Again all my fault.

It was still costing me money just to end this relationship and to get totally free.

It is very important for you to consider what getting into a relationship of this type will cost you. Know that you are taking a chance and no one really knows the outcome, so if you really don't mind giving money that you will never see again and never get repaid for, it is up to you, but don't expect it back, and this is also true of whatever you give in the name of love.

Some men will say, "She wanted me so bad, she just gave me money, or because we were dating, I don't think I have to pay her back."

So if you give, don't even expect to get it back! Count it as a loss.

My job began to cut my hours immediately after I made my transition from my man and my finances were in total disarray. I was really robbing Peter to pay Paul as they say, and cut-off notices were everywhere in the mail on a daily basis. To this day, I am still paying for my unwise decision to bring this man into my life and to take care of him.

All of this came as a result of excessive spending, going to different leasing companies to borrow money putting myself deeper in debt, mismanagement of record keeping caused checks to begin to bounce like dominos, trying to keep him happy by meeting all of his needs and desires all on my salary alone.

This man put me through and I deserved this for allowing it by giving him my money and making things so easy for him. I can't get mad at him or even hate him for what I was so determined to do for him. I set myself up for this hurt and disappointment, he just took advantage of an opportunity,

I can learn from this bitter experience and never be found in this position again, I will survive this. I am sorry things turned out like this, but I am grateful for a lesson learned and I am free, free to the point that I will not be a FOOL for a man again.

Here I am, I just put him out of my life and now I am gathering up all of the coins I can find, yes, It has come down to this, change, I am searching in the corners of all of my dresser drawers, coat pockets, corners of the couch and it all comes up to pennies and dimes. All of my money was spent on him, where is all that money I spent on him? How much did I spend? Oh, what does it matter now, I can't even tell you how much it was so much!

Oh, God, please let me find just enough change to get me something to eat for dinner today. He doesn't have to worry, he lives

My Desperate Search For Love

back at home with his mother and he eats out of her pots everyday and he doesn't have to pay rent, he doesn't even have to get up if he doesn't want to. What a wasted life. Well, I can't worry about that now, I am just trying to get some dinner for today.

I have just enough gas to get to the store and I am praying that it will be enough to get me back and fourth to work this week, until Friday when I get paid. Well, I have what I want some instant noodles and a can of soup, I sure hope I have enough to pay for this, Maybe it will add up to $5.00, I sure hope it doesn't go over.

I was so embarrassed at the check out counter, because people were huffing and puffing behind me, because the line was getting longer and longer and I was standing there counting all of this change hoping to have five dollars and I felt the pressure and I turned and looked at all of them and I could see the hatred in their eyes because I was inconveniencing their lives by taking so long, but I looked back at them with bloodshot eyes that had become red from crying all night for the past week because my life had been inconvenienced by a man I chose to love, who did not chose to love me back, who had just too many other issues.

I stood there trying to get this change together and it represented all I was left with for my foolish and unwise decision to put his needs first, pennies that's all it came down to pennies. Some people sneered, others laughed so hard and I felt like one of the homeless, who had been put in their position beyond their control and I became overwhelmed because I could not count the change fast enough, I have never been so hurt, or embarrassed in my life!

I felt how cold and heartless can these people be, don't they know it was the end of the world I thought would end in possibility of marriage or at least a long lasting union, don't they know what has happened to me, of course not and nobody even cared except God.

I stood there as if in a state of BANKRUPTCY and I was— Emotionally Bankrupt and Financially Bankrupt and I had no more to give.

I looked up with tears in my eyes at the check-out clerk who looked at me as if she knew what I had been through and she said, That's OK honey, I'll put up the money for you, and she began to give me all of the coins back and smiled at me and touched my *hands gently, as if to say, I understand as she rang everything up and I was speechless.*

When I walked out of the store I said this to the Lord:
MY SOUL IS IN DEEP DESPAIR, OH GOD, OH GOD, PLEASE HELP ME, I HAVE NEVER BEEN DOWN SO LOW BEFORE!
LORD, I PUT THIS MAN FIRST, EVEN BEFORE YOU AND I HAVE GIVEN ALL OF MY MONEY TO TRY AND MAKE HIM LOVE ME AND TO HELP HIS LIFE AND I HAVE COME UP EMPTY, EVEN AFTER ALL I GAVE, I AM EMPTY!
FORGIVE ME, AND PLEASE HELP ME!
MY SOUL FEELS LIKE I AM IN THE BOTTOM OF THE DARKEST PIT, WHERE NO LIGHT IS.
LORD, I NEED YOUR HELP RIGHT NOW!

Later, when I got home, I cried, cried, and cried some more, but God gave me the strength and he let me see that even though I created this situation and it was by my own doing, he was going to deliver me out and help me.

God also showed me that I was going to suffer from the consequences of my actions, because with each action or road we make a decision to follow, He could not remove the consequences, but that I would learn a life-long lesson from this experience and that I will never be found here again.

I thanked God through my tears and my pain, Thank you Lord, Thank you Lord. It could have been worse, I could still be just like I was.

I did this to myself when I began to hold this person responsible for making me happy and for allowing him to take the place in my life and trying to make him love me for the things I gave and did, when God already loves me with a deeper lover than any man can give me without cost or favors.

My situation could not change until I got tired and said, Hey, Enough is Enough and I can bear it no longer!! I had to put a stop to it! Some things don't take a Rocket Scientist to show you what is up, and we don't need to ask God to help us out or to stop it, we can put and end to some of this stuff our ownselves, be we do need His strength, but we already have his love and He is more than willing to help us get free, if we want it!

To my dear Sisters and to anyone who reads this book, When you are in a relationship, friendship or marriage that is DRAINING you and vexing your soul and the person is not adding anything to your life, but instead tearing you down and you are doing all of the giving and he is doing all of the taking, IT IS TIME TO GO!!!!

MY REAL VIEW OF MY MAN

In all fairness to my man and others like him, I began to realize that they are the true VICTIMS.

We Must Pray for our men!

We must also help build up and restore our men and teach them through the love of God, just how to be men again.

Looking back over my experience with my man, through the eyes of love, I saw that it was because of the poor foundation that I laid that resulted in a horrible outcome.

If the foundation is flawed, the whole structure will be flawed!

The way you start a relationship is the foundation.

The foundation carries the weight and the load of the entire structure or the relationship.

The key to the effectiveness, stability and the strength is what the foundation is made up of.

In my foundation of my relationship, I started with very poor and weak materials. I completely compromised all of my principles taught to me by my Mother and by God for the sake of saying, I got me a man now!

My desire for my man made me take leave of all of my good sense, he looked so good to my eyes and I only cared about what I saw and I got carried away and caught up with infatuation.

My man is free of guilt or blame and so are many other men. We women will cast all decency to the wind and throw ourselves at you without respect for ourselves and no shame in our game.

I am guilty of this. My foundation began with me setting my sights on this man and I was going to do whatever it took to make him happy and make him mine.

I became the man, like a hunter after his prey, I totally casted all of my lady-like teachings and morals. Men should be the pursuers, not the women and that's another problem with my foundation.

I took it upon myself to be his rescuer and provider by paying for everything at the beginning. Remember if you start it this way, it is expected to continue this way.

Women, we are armed and dangerous because many of us make more money than our men and we use our money as power to control and manipulate our men by providing their needs and wants.

I used my power to buy everything, pay for all of our dinners, lunches, movies until it was just the norm, but remember I volunteered to do it and because I had it like that, I was happy to do it, So I can't put the blame on him.

Many times when we were out to dinner, I would pass the money under the table to make it appear that he was paying for things to make him look good.

The reason why our relationship lasted six years, was because even though I built a horrible foundation, he was also a decent man and I felt special when I was with him. He was very respectable. He did many favors for me in return for my financial help, like painting my apartment, fixing anything that needed to be fixed, washing and waxing my car, taking out the garbage, and rising to the occasion whenever I needed a real man to handle things.

We did have some very good times together. We both enjoyed movies and television and we were forever in video stores.

I truly enjoyed his companionship. He never fronted with me and told me several times that he did not love me, but I would simply shrug it off and I figured if I do enough for him, maybe, just maybe, he will fall in love with me.

This is another bad problem in the foundation I laid. I didn't realize how much I was hurting him by doing so much for him.

I had a good job and I didn't want my man to suffer or lack anything, especially when I could help him with what he needed.

Here again is a point of victimization for our men. We cause them to become dependent upon us and they won't do for themselves *and why should they when we are going to provide it.*

This is robbing a man of his manhood and many of us women think that because we are doing this for you, you should love us and do whatever we want and become whatever we want you to become.

This is a problem that is currently at an epidemic proportion.

This adds to an already faulty foundation of a total Role-Reversal.

Who's the Man? We Women are the Man, that's who!

I WANTED TO BE YOUR LOVER, NOT YOUR MOTHER!

Even though I will take responsibility for trying to play "Santa Clause," by giving to my man, I will not leave my man without taking on any part in creating this situation.

I should not have had to go through trying to make a man get up out of bed and go to work or to be responsible.

When men act like little boys, they make us act like their Mothers. Why should we have to tell you how to be a man?

You should come into a relationship bringing to the table or at least maintaining your own needs and financial responsibility so that we can be more comfortable and each of us will not feel threatened by the notion that someone is trying to "Mooch off of us" or play us.

We are living in hard times and no one can carry their bills and responsibilities and yours too.

I just wanted to be a partner, a girlfriend, not a Mother. You already have a Mother, you didn't need two.

When a man doesn't carry his own weight, he causes us to have to step in and assist in his life.

The number one cause of broken marriages and relationships is financial.

When each person maintains their own business and finances, we are free from stress and then we can concentrate on the romantic, intimate and emotional areas of our relationship, in short, we can love each other.

So men, you need to handle your business, so we won't have to.

HOW DID THIS HAPPEN?

I am glad for all of my brothers and sisters, but I was the eighth child born and then there would be a total of 17 of us. This played a great deal in shaping my personality because I was not special.

Once born I feel into a group situation and became one of the pack, so to speak. I love each of my family members, I am only saying that I had no sense of singleness and received no individual attention and I completely understood the situation, but that doesn't mean that I didn't long for more private and personal time with each of my parents, because I did long to be nearer to them and be special to them.

I am not crying over spilt milk or wishing I was an only child by no means, I am simply saying I realize that what I didn't get then, I will never get it, that time has passed, but God has shown me that His love is a healer to my soul and so powerful that it can fill the void of past love longed for.

I guess it started when I was a child wanting to be liked and accepted when I attended school by the other school children. I remember doing all kind of favors, giving gifts to win their friendship and approval.

This started out in kindergarten and lasted even throughout high school.

I was always going out of my way to give my class mates presents on their birthday and cards- you name it, I'll try to do it or find a way to get it for you.

It was a very sad eye-opener to realize that they were not my friends at all. They knew I wanted to be accepted and they used the opportunity of my vulnerability to get the things they needed. When the giving ran out, so did the phony friendships.

I know now that the desire to be loved and to belong can drive you in every area of your life.

All you know is this driving force that seeks every opportunity to get acceptance and approval.

This same spirit carried over into my involvement with a church I began to attend.

Before I knew it, I was trying to work for my salvation. I was so grateful to God for giving His son Jesus, I tried to earn it. I found myself on every church committee, in every ministry to feed this desire and hunger to repay God.

Now you know you can't pay for your salvation, but I sure did try. You talk about tired. I was worn out. I would put all of my needs on hold and my personal needs, housework, laundry, errands were all on hold until the Lord's work was done.

Don't misunderstand me, working for the Church is a very good thing, but what I was doing was abnormal. We have to be careful that we are doing God's will, God's way.

Sometimes we are doing things that God did not ask us to do. There is a point where you can become so heavenly holy that you are no earthly good, and that is how I became to the point of getting sick and wearing myself out.

Before I came to my realization, I found myself a member of a small prayer group, which had very striking similarities of control and domination that were similar to the profile of a cult. This organization had very strict rules for our personal and private lives supposedly for the will and the purpose of God and for our spiritual growth and enhancement.

I don't want to sound bitter or to blame the organization, in the beginning they were very good to me and I am grateful for all of the things I learned and experienced.

I must keep it real, because I was the one in a desperate search for love and acceptance and they were there for me, but this was again my fault because of that spirit in me to try to buy and earn my acceptance and gain a sense of belonging.

I do not blame them for the weaknesses of my spirit to try and be a part of the prayer group and desperately seeking to fit in. I again take the blame.

It began very positive and once again I began to pour myself into it everything I had, and felt very blessed to be a part of this group, but my joy soon turned into fear, sorrow and deep regret. I would cry and be nervous all of the time, so much so that my emotional and physical health began to suffer.

I worked twice as hard as I had for the church and found myself only getting two to three hours of sleep a day. I would be so tired when I laid down that I would wet the bed, yes a grown woman wetting the bed because I slept so sound, plus I had a weak bladder and never felt the pressure to go when it was time.

I would teach a class in the evening after working all day and I was going through this rigorous and draining routine and was so tired that I feel asleep at my desk which was in the front of the students. You can only imagine my horror to awaken with over 30 adult students looking at me.

I was so ashamed, embarrassed and full of humiliation and wondered how could I let this happen to myself.

I gained weight through a lot of stress and overeating, since they controlled our intake of food and had us fasting extensively, so me and the other members would sneak and eat.

The thing that I originally loved and gave up all to be a part of, became the thing I hated and I wanted out. I was eventually told that because I had gained so much weight, that I no longer looked professional and was told that I needed to leave.

Just like that, to leave. I had given up all of my family and friends to solely focus and dedicate myself to this cause and organization for thirteen (13) years and all in one day, you tell me to leave.

I was glad to count up my losses and this was my gateway to freedom. I ran like a slave leaving a life of slavery and bondage, set free from Masas' Plantation (Ebonics).

See how this spirit carries over into everything.

Finally, after Thirteen (13) years I was free, Thank God.

During all of these years, I was faithful to God and I loved and honored Him, and His word and His Spirit kept me. I was so faithful

My Desperate Search For Love

to God's work and was so sincere, I did not even as much as date or talk to men on the phone, nor had I slept with any man.

So once free from this bondage and this organization, I felt that it was time for me. I turned my back on God's ways concerning fornication and wanted desperately to be loved and to be in a relationship with a man.

Let's just keep it real, wouldn't you want to experience everything you missed after feeling you have given all of your time, years of your life only to have it washed down the drain. I was very confused and felt that this time is mine.

I was angry over the years of service, which I might add, were all voluntary, there was no steady salary, only handouts of a menial allotment for personal products and needs.

I know it is wrong now, but then I said, God, I love you and I am sorry, but I got to find me a man now and I got to enjoy my life.

This is where my search became a desperate one.

I was headed for trouble like a runaway train on an endless track.

My self-esteem was so low and I was so hungry for male companionship, that I had no standards or criteria. At this point, anyone would do.!

I accepted all type of men.

Let me give you a brief rundown to show you how messed up my head was.

These men, I will not name, but I will briefly describe.

First there was one who lived in a hotel, who rode the bus, nice body, but no direction or goals.

Next there was a scrubb, No car, no money, no job—wanted to make love and watch TV.

Next a male dancer with 7 children who lived at home with Mom.

Next the murderer, who had just been released and got my number from a friend, who could not keep a job because of his offense.

Next the bartender, no car, no phone, no goals, and thought he was God's gift.

Next a Muslim, who was getting divorced, very nice decent and treated me like a lady with respect, but wanted a Muslim woman and always wanted to sell me things. He wanted to make love but did not want any type of commitment.

Next a very slow man who lived with Moma and she controlled him and he had no car or phone of his own and always had to wait for his cousin to bring him my way.

Next a bus driver, who had his own house but never took me to it, drove a corvette and a 4 x 4 and never took me out in it. He always came over after hours, after his shift (Booty Call). He was a gentleman, but wanted nothing other than sex and always begged to let him set up a video camera so he could tape our lovemaking.

Next a mentally challenged man. It was a blind date. He had a car, job and was a gentleman, but not all there. He was innocent and very childlike and at the end of movies he would applaud like a baby.

I said to myself, now you have stooped to an all-time low.

Next there was the Jigalow who posed as a man who loved large women and was fine, polished and professional without a car, phone, or a job. First he was between jobs and just needed a hand-out until he got on his feet, which never seemed to happen, at least while we were together. Unfortunately, I assisted him financially and was constantly harassed for more and more money. He was a milker and I woke up in time and cut him off with a quickness, while he was waiting for me to express mail his rent, which he is still waiting on it.

Next there was the mortician—Almost the most promising, but no car and rented a room, but true gentlemen and true deceiver, who wanted to borrow my car right away for his own purposes and ran up an enormous bill with my mechanic for a car he wanted to buy and then called my house and asked me to take a check to my mechanic and he would pay me later. He was a user and felt that his charm and charisma would get him anywhere. I paid my mechanic, but not for him, but because I had referred him and he messed over my friend. After that, I never cared to call him again. He thinks he got over, but I got free after seeing him for what he was.

This brings us to the current man in my search.

Let me say that I am not trying to dog or make brothers look bad, remember I am only trying to point out how low my esteem was and that I really didn't have any standards or stipulations—I was open to everyone, and I must say that even though I have *known a lot of different men, each one of them taught me something about myself and added to my life.*

So, they took something from me and I took from them as well.

There are very good men who can be down on their luck and they may be fixer-uppers, but none of these were.

I am not happy about my past, but that is just what it is THE PAST.

So I really can't blame just one man for my current state.

We need to be careful of our overly kind nature, our inner need to love so strongly that we are willing to do anything to be loved, because we set ourselves up without even knowing it.

Each of us send a message and signals about how we feel about ourselves, so be careful and ask yourself, What kind of message am I sending?

HOW DID I GET THIS WAY?

We all may have different reasons because we all have different experiences from our past.

I guess it started when I was a child wanting to be liked so badly by the other school children that I would go special favors like share my school supplies and my lunch, as well as, give them gifts. This behavior began as early as kindergarten and continued up until High School.

I was always going out of my way to earn their friendship and approval.

It was very sad, but eye opening to realize that they really weren't my friends, they were just using me, and when the giving gave out, so did their phony friendship.

This desire to belong and to be loved can drive you in every area of your life. All you know is this driving force that seeks out every opportunity to get acceptance and approval.

This same spirit and force carried over into an association with the church I began to attend. Before I knew it, I was on every committee and assisting in every ministry to feed that desire to be a part and to be accepted.

You talk about TIRED. I was worn out! Don't misunderstand me, working in the church was very positive, but I was overdoing it and God had not called me to do all of this, to the point of wearing myself thin and it wearing myself out.

I was so full of zeal I also joined a small private prayer band, which was not a cult, but it was just as rigorous and as strict with rules and regulations for our spiritual enhancement.

It started out so beautiful and positive and I felt so blessed to be a part of this unique organization, but my joy soon turned to sorrow and deep regret.

I was under intense pressure and scrutiny and had to give an account of my every action twenty-four hours of everyday. I had to report every activity I was involved in and I was watched all of the time.

My focus was simply to be on the work of God and I was to ignore my family and focus on this work and mission for God. Thinking that I was doing what God wanted me to do, I dove in with all I had, working night and day for this cause, which we served in the community as a Christian Computer Training School.

So I was fully committed starting my day with cleaning the school facilities, as a janitor then teaching from 8:30 am until 2:30 pm, then I took to the streets to go recruiting or collecting donations. This would go on until time to return to the school to teach an evening session from 8:00 pm, until 10:00 pm. I also made time to recruit in all of the local shelters and homes for battered women, sometimes picking up new recruits to get food, clothing and helping them to find shelter.

I would be so tired, nervous and scared that I was not pleasing God and the school administrators, who were Missionaries, that I would find my nerves were shot. One time I worked so hard until I feel into a deep sleep, so deep that I could not feel my body trying to signal me to go to the bathroom and I wet the bed. I always had a weak bladder and had bedwetting occurrences from time to time in my life, but it began to happen on a regular basis.

I was so tired one evening while instructing a class, I feel asleep in front of a whole class of students. The embarrassment was horrific and I was ordered to go home. I gained weight due to stress eating and was fired due to my obesity and openly humiliated while teaching class, one of the administrators came in and said, Maybe the students could see the chalk board, if your big body wasn't in the way!

What seemed to be a firing to me meant my badge of freedom and I wore that badge with pride and I ran like a slave set free from

Massah's Plantation.

Finally, after 13 years of dedicated service to this organization, I Was FREE.

During these years, I was faithful to God and to this cause. I did not date, talk on the phone to men, nor slept with any man. I know it seems hard to believe, but it is true. God's spirit kept me clean and pure and I lived my life as a Nun or Missionary because I wanted God to use me.

So once freed, I said to myself, Now It Is Time For Me!!!

I was very angry over all of the years I had dedicated, served and worked as a volunteer and pissed off, so I to myself, I got to hurry up and find me a man so I could make up for lost time and try to enjoy my life now.

My self-esteem at this point was very low and I had not been aware of how the times had changed with dating and meeting a man. At this point, I was not about to take years to get to know someone because I had to resolve my problem of not having been with a man for so long, that I really had no standards. ANY MAN WILL DO!!

As mentioned in my previous chapter, I accepted men with no phone, no car, no real interest other than having sex, men who had criminal records, I even ended up dating a murderer, even a man who was on the slow side, so you can see my search really did turn desperate.

REASONS THIS HAPPENED

*W*henever you decide to believe a lie instead of the truth, you and only you, open up the door to deception into your heart. Don't make things what they aren't in a relationship.

I know that I saw a lot of signs in my past relationships, but I chose not to face them, I went into denial.

If all you do is take care of a man as I did, by meeting all of his needs, financial, sexual, mentally, emotional, material, whatever, ask yourself what kind of relationship you will have if you stop?

Ask yourself another question, If you are doing everything, What is he doing for you?

Don't rationalize and try to give a good justifiable reason for your actions.

This is one of the main reasons my situation was created.

Rationalizing and reasoning are also part of a fairy tale illusion and by doing this, you begin to spin a web of blindness that you will go deeper into.

You begin to reason like I did: Here are some Examples:

- *He is just so misunderstood by his family and friends, and no one understands him like me.*
- *He has just had a bad break and such a terrible childhood.*
- *I am only helping him until he gets on his feet.*
- *When he gets himself together, he will pay me back every penny.*
- *If I don't help him, he won't make it and no one will help him.*

- *He is just down and out for right now.*
- *If I do these things for him, Surely, I'll make him love me*

All of these previously mentioned rationales got me into my big mess!

It helped me to create a world of my own that existed only in my mind and in my mind alone.

Don't we call people who create their own little world CRAZY?

I AM GOING TO MAKE HIM LOVE ME!

*I*n my case, it was six years of sacrificing and believing, I know he loves me now, that my man came to me, while I was grieving over the death of my dearly departed mother and wallowing deep in pain that he said these words to me:

I love being around you and hanging out with you and all that, but I DON'T LOVE YOU, I can't return all of the emotion and passion you give to me.

At this moment, my world literally stopped! I felt for the first time that the hands of time actually stood in as state of suspended animation with stillness!

Maybe it is because I was already in the valley of sorrow for my mother, I don't know what made me hear him, but I heard his message loud and clear. His timing could not be more off. Before I could get over the fatal blow of my mother's death, he hit me with another one, right in my gut.

I felt the pain and I heard the words, but I looked with amazement asking how can you say this to me at this tumultuous time? How cold and heartless can you be! Why now? Why Me?

I received no consoling, not a rose, not a flower, not a hug, not even a sympathy card!

I was stunned, shocked and simply devastated!

I really can't fault my man because before this time, he tried to tell me, but I was so determined that I was going to make him love *me, I never really heard him. I was so dead set on trying to make him love me, I did not listen to him, but I get it now, I really get it now.*

He kept trying to tell me by some of the things he did, his actions were so clear, but I overrode them, saying things to myself like, He doesn't really mean it, I'll just overlook him, he doesn't know what he needs, I do.

I was so determined to stay in darkness without knowing it.

Look for the signs, They are there, don't overlook them.

My man would sometimes sleep on the couch when we finished making love and sometimes he would tell me cruel things like stop touching me because I can't sleep.

He would also ignore my calls on his cell phone and ignore my paging.

He would disappear for days at a time and then show up like nothing happened.

He got to the point where he wouldn't show any type of emotion, but he still wanted to have sex, without kissing or any type of foreplay or cuddling, just that cold hearted—Slam, bam, thank you man type of sex.

Sometimes he would come over like he wanted to see me and then ask for money and then leave.

Sometimes he would call while hanging out with his boys and promise to come over and never show up.

I made a conscious decision to let this relationship go and accepted the fact that it was over.

WHAT MY EXPERIENCE TAUGHT ME

I LEARNED I WAS WRONG

*M*y experience taught me that I brought a lot of unnecessary DRAMA on myself, solely because I was dead set and determined on making this man mine.

I failed to accept or even consider the fact that this may not be the man God had for me.

A major decision like this needs God's direction and guidance.

We are clearly out of order as women, God's word tells us "He that findeth a wife, Findeth a good thing."

We have stepped out of order by chasing the man, instead of letting the man do the choosing.

We also bring hurt, problems, devastation and sorrow to our lives, and we end up with men God has not chosen for us.

We then get so caught up at how good looking he is and sexually satisfied, that we become as if one who is **"BRAIN DEAD."**

We seem to fall into a state of "Temporary Insanity."

Now that you have taken leave of all of your senses, then the next thing you know, you are doing some or all of the following things:

—Giving him money and accepting the fact that he doesn't work.
—Buying him a cell phone to talk to him more.
—Moving him into your apartment or home without any assistance for rent, mortgage or bills.
—Treating him like he is our husband, cooking, cleaning and having their babies, becoming a Baby's Momma and making him a Baby's Daddy.
—Give him our car to ride around all day, with no job, so he can drop us off and pick us up.
—Giving him our body to keep him sexually satisfied and we feel that they are doing us such a big favor as well.
—We take on all of their problems, helping them get out of jail, assist with paying child support payments for babies fathered out of other relationships.
—We will work two jobs while he stays at home, eating our food and running up our electricity, gas and cable bill by ordering pay-per view movies.
—Some of us leave our babies with these men to be abused, killed or tortured, whether he is the father or not.
—Many of us put our jobs in jeopardy, taking days off in order to stay home with him, since he doesn't work.
—We allow our credit to be destroyed by co-signing for cars, cell phones, buying them clothes, getting utilities turned on in their names and the list goes on and on!

The point I am trying to make is that we do this all in the name of LOVE!

Many of us start out innocently trying to help our men out, hoping that they will be grateful enough to fall in love with us, and want to become a part of our lives.

Some people may call women like this Stupid, but it really is not just that. There is a real sincere hunger for love and acceptance and no one does something without expecting something in return.

It is not stupid to siincerely love and care for someone, and it is not stupid to desire love and acceptance, but to try to buy a man's love is futile and fruitless.

Many of us see what is going on, but in denial, we say to ourselves, "Just hang in their a little longer. It will get better. So just stay with him."

This lie will be easy to accept, because of all of the things you have already done for them and you will feel that you have invested too much into this person to let them go.

Your weakness and blindness will also make you come up with logical reasons why you do all of the things you do for them and develop a sense of importance believing that he really needs you.

We must Wake Up and realize that this is all a result of a lack of love, a lack of knowing your self-worth and value, but especially our lack of self-esteem and not knowing who you are in God.

We must restore order and let God free us from this Co-dependent Spirit, and return to Him as our true love of our live.

We must stop this crazy self-destructive obsession over men who don't love us and are just using us because we allow them to do it.

THE BREAKING POINT

*E*ach woman has a breaking point and no one can tell you anything until you reach yours.

No one knows just what will be the straw that will break the camel's back, but the camel because he is the one bearing the load and only he knows when the load is too much to continue to carry.

God can and will free you of your load and heavy burden that you have allowed to come upon you, if you truly want to be free.

If you stay in a "Dead-End Relationship," you are just wasting your time!

If you are reading this book and you fit this profile, and are tired of the DRAMA, God is speaking to your heart to let you know you can be free right now.

You've tried everything else and still not found happiness, now open your heart to God and ask Him to forgive you of your sins and totally surrender to Him and seek Him for the love of your life that he originally established for you to have.

Love yourself enough to end this <u>**destructive cycle.**</u>
<u>You've tried the rest, Now try the Best!</u>

GOD WANTS TO GIVE YOU HIS BEST, WON'T YOU LET HIM?

*R*emember, *don't be too hard on yourself, because it is all a part of life and life is a process. We live and we make mistakes and then we learn not to repeat them again. We did not get into our situation over night and it will take some time to recover and to get back to normal.*

Many of us will have to suffer some consequences for our actions, but God can fix any situation and these **Broken Wings can fly again!!!**

There is nothing too hard for God to fix, even our Broken lives because he is the Potter who wants to put us back together again!!!

Let's let our journey to discovering God's plan and Will for our lives begin now as we walk into our freedom from bondage.

<u>**GOD LOVES YOU AND CAME TO RESCUE YOU BECAUSE YOU ARE TO HIM, A PEARL OF GREAT PRICE!!!!**</u>

THE "K E P T" MAN

*M*y *man was not evil, vindictive or mean, I appreciated that and he did what he could for me and I appreciated him for that.*

My man did, however, even though he did not say it verbally, expected to be a "Kept" Man.

This is a man who feels that they are so badly needed and that they are so fine, sexually endowed and gorgeous that they are a treasure and a vitally needed asset to any financially stable, hard-working woman who is so lonely, desperate, hard-up, lustful, got-to-have-a-man-around type of woman.

JUST HOW DID THESE MEN GET THIS WAY? YOU ASK?
WE MADE THEM THAT WAY!!!!!!

It is sad to say, but true. We pick right up where Momma left off and in some cases, they may still be at Momma's.

This is a monster that we created as women. I am just as guilty.

Many of us give off the wrong signals, and I know I did when I met my man. It seemed as if I had this desperate, lonely longing on my face and a lot of times we don't even know we are giving this type of signal.

This type of man knows how badly you want them, because we either tell them or let them know it, and we also show our willingness to do anything and everything for them.

Be very careful of the message that you are sending. We must be careful to realize that we unknowingly send out a message in our conversation, actions and mannerisms.

Some of us put our business in the street and give what my friends call T. M. I.—Too Much Information.

Our signs are there and being picked up just like a radio signal, unfortunately by the wrong kind of man.

This type of man can pick us up a mile away and I was picked up by my man. I was excited to meet him and swept away with him and was overtaken by his handsomeness and charm.

I made the decision that I wanted and needed his company. I worked hard and I considered him a special treat that I was giving to myself and while I had it, I didn't mind helping him.

In the beginning of your friendship/relationship, this will not bother you, but after the same old thing happening of him being broke, can't find work, won't even get out of bed and go look for work and you are continuing to carry the load alone, you will become resentful.

Becoming resentful and angry are only natural reactions because you begin to feel used, played, being taken for granted.

It is unreasonable and unhealthy for one person to look at another to be the sole source of all their needs and it is an abomination in the sight of God for an able-bodied man, who begins to show you that he won't work and after you have tried to help him get on his feet, refuses to even try to find work and he still expects you to carry the load.

I am guilty of starting the relationship off on the wrong foot and then when I got tired, it was too late for change. I had created this situation, so I could not get mad or bitter, but I began to see just how serious and dangerous this was for not only my man, but for all men.

We as women must see that this is hurting our men for us to assume the dominant role; this was never the intention of God.

Having gone down this road, please let me warn you before you and all other women begin to believe that this is an acceptable behavior.

Just because society says this is a new day, doesn't make it the right way. I want a real man. I want a man to be a man and I am not trying to challenge him for his position.

We both can't be the man, nor can we both be the woman. I am looking for us to work together to equally bring something to the table and in today's economic state; it takes two just to live comfortably.

Again, be careful how you lay your foundation in the very beginning, because if it starts off wrong, guess what, it will be too far gone to correct.

If a man did not have to do the right thing to get you, he sure won't have to change and do the right thing to keep you.

Many of us have worked so hard to make our relationships work, that we got caught up in trying to meet our man's needs for acceptance and approval, hoping to win his love and affection.

Some of us, and I know that I am guilty of this, used his state of neediness as an opportunity to buy a place in his heart and secure us a place in his life. It is sad to say, but we took advantage of their down period in their life to make them become dependent on us.

It is wrong for us to take their sense of manhood and their purpose for being a provider, protector and head of the household away to meet our selfish needs in wanting them.

We are only fooling ourselves to try and convince ourselves that going against an established order taught by our mothers and taking leave our good common sense, and moral values is O.K.

Trying to do your part and his part is too hard. We can do it for a while, but we will get tired. Then when we stop doing it after we have them dependent upon us to, nothing gets done.

This is where the real "Drama" begins.

Our man's attitude begins to change toward us when we can no longer keep up this routine.

We realize then, when we stop doing all the work, our relationship begins to go sour, or we become so tired and frustrated for being expected to be the breadwinner, we don't even care any more. We just want out because we are in need of some care and some pampering our own selves.

WHEN HELPING SOMEONE IS REALLY HURTING THEM

*D*oing all of the work in a relationship is not love. I was not helping my man by taking the initiative to do everything for him.

I was creating a dependency on me and robbing him of his opportunity to participate in his own success.

I was stripping him of his purpose for being a man when I took control. If an able bodied person sits around and watches you kill yourself day in and day out, and offers no help or assistance, they don't love you either to watch you suffer and work like a dog.

We have love confused and this misconception is getting us into a lot of trouble.

We are nurturing by nature and God help you men when our "Mothering Instincts" kick in. We will mother you to death and become controlling, but only because we think we know what is best for you and because we care, I know, I did it too.

Men must share the blame for this as well. If you act like a little boy, then I have to treat you like I am your Mother, and it is because you put me in that situation. I am your lover, not your Mother!

My intent to help my man was sincere; I did not know that I was hurting him. I was robbing him of his responsibility to feel important and to feel needed.

No matter how positive or sincere your rationale for doing this, it is never going to meet with positive results.

This is self-defeating and will destroy a relationship in time. By

My Desperate Search For Love

your doing for your man, you are enabling him to be irresponsible by not requiring that he does his share. This is where we begin to feel victimized.

The end results will always be negative; the formula always yields the same results.

My financial security became so shot, because I tried to handle my financial affairs and my man's too.

I never anticipated that I would be expected to continue carrying the load and I was in hope of receiving some help or at least hoping that he would begin carrying his own load.

My downfall started with me making constant and excessive withdrawals from my checking account and writing numerous checks prior to my regular paydays. Needless to say, checks began bouncing everywhere, 4 and 5 at a time, and with each insufficient check, a charge of $25.

So I had the $25 charge, in addition to making the check good, and an additional bounced check fee with the person the check was originally written to. Sometimes I couldn't track the check in time and it would hit the bank for the second time adding another $25.

I also made sure I always had money on me in case my man needed any, so I would borrow from cash leasing companies, sometimes $300 to $500 at a time.

I had maintained all of this by working overtime, but then my job cut my hours and that is when the bottom fell out for me!

Suddenly, I owed more than I was making and I had no help from my man because he could not keep a job long enough or he just didn't have a chance to do any handiwork.

I began to see the truth, that I had become a **"Caretaker"** for someone, who could not take care of me or offer me any assistance when I needed it, because I was responsible for hindering him and guilty of not requiring him to do his share.

I could not live like this anymore.

My mistake was trying to be the man, carry the load and not sharing with my man about how bad things really were. While it is true that it didn't take a Rocket Scientist to know we needed money, I never disclosed with my man what I had to do to maintain my status. I was so busy fronting with him and trying to look like Ms. Super

Girl, he really did not know what I was doing to keep him happy.

I made one final attempt to help my man get a job, and this time it really paid off! He was hired at a very prestigious firm, definitely a fortune-five hundred company and I was so happy for him. I told him that I could no longer carry him and that he was now responsible for all of his own needs. I made good on my promise.

I was so happy for him and proud, but I was also relieved to be free.

Carrying myself, I began to re-build my checking account and paying off other bills that were overdue, as well as, paying off the cash leasing companies.

I knew whatever we had, it was over because I built the relationship on his dependency on me, so his getting a job was like letting a bird free from his cage, so in essence, we both got free.

My man stopped calling and coming by as I had expected he would. He would check in with me from time to time and tell me all of the new things he bought for himself and he was so happy to be able to buy whatever he wanted.

I wanted nothing but the best for him and never made any demands on any monies that I spent on him. I just wanted him to be self-sufficient and on his own, so in a way, we both won.

I am sorry to say that this happiness was short-lived. He was on his feet, at least a little while, the total sum of four months and then he was fired for not showing up one day and he also did not call in.

I would later learn that he was out drinking with his buddies and he was unable to get up and go in.

I was so sorry that he lost his job, but I could no longer offer any aid or assistance as I had in the past. I was not able to carry him any longer. He was no longer my responsibility and he should have never been anyway.

We do not have the ability to change another, *we can only change ourselves.*

I have changed because I want to help our men be men again and not offer them crutches or wheel chairs when they can walk for themselves.

I will always care about him, but I can no longer allow myself to be in the same position as I was. I am wrong for helping him so much, but my motive was sincere and no matter what happens, he will always maintain a special place in my heart and in my memory.

I am grateful to God for my lesson learned.

I am stronger now. I still have emotional scars, but I am not willing to get in that situation again, I am not willing to lose my security and financial stability again, for the love of a man, and especially if this person is not my husband and with God's help and guidance, I will never have to!

SMELLING THE "COFFEE"

To all my Girls, Ladies, Homegirls, Sisters, Women, and females of every race, creed, color, sizes, shapes, etc.
SMELLING THE COFFEE—THIS IS HARD– OKAY!
Smelling the Coffee is hard because love is blind and you are so taken and blown away with how fine and cute he is and how good his sex is to you that you go into denial, willingly blinding yourself.

I an not happy about it, but it happens to us all.

I don't know about you, but looking back at my life, I feel like I was in a coma or a state when I just couldn't think straight.

While in this state, I ignored all of his faults, former jail time, tickets, illegitimate children and believed whatever he told me.

I ignored the truth, but the saddest thing is that you can cover up and hide and fool others, **but you can't fool yourself**.

My motive may have been sincere, but the outcome was damaging to my man and me. I was wrong and my motive was wrong.

I was using him to fulfill a void that was in me and felt that he could fill it. I would help him and in turn gain a sense of value for being needed.

Once I saw his areas of weakness, whether they be financial, emotional or whatever, I would have a secure and solid place in his life by helping to meet any of the above needs.

I know this sounds sick, but I felt that if I met his needs, he would somehow give me what I needed. Women, you know I am not alone on this one, let's be real with ourselves!

God showed me I created this situation by striking out on my *own, without even seeking his advice or consulting him concerning His will, to the point of asking "Is this the man you meant for me to be with, not just for the purpose of being a boyfriend for the rest of my life, God never intends for any of us to date all of our lives, nor for the purpose of just "Shacking Up," living together, but for the purpose of marriage.*

God began to show me that I abandoned all that I knew that was right in His eyes, to get what I waned, not what He had ordained and wanted for me.

First of all, you need to open your heart to God for direction, Secondly, you must love yourself and learn how to be a whole person, as a single person and then you will not gauge your worth and value based on another's opinion of you.

YOUR EMOTIONAL FALLOUT

When your emotions kick in after this experience and they will, your first reaction is hurt, intense anger and you feel, **"This isn't fair,"** and sometimes life isn't fair.

I also feel that men have a responsibility to be truthful and honest in the beginning and to tell us they don't want us, but only what we have to offer, but the point of my book is that we are so bent and determined on making them love us, would we really hear them?

I feel so sorry for women I see on TV on these Judge Shows that are trying to recover what they have given to their man and the women will say "I loaned him" and the men will say, she was my girlfriend and "It was a GIFT."

How embarrassing to think you are in love and to have someone think that you are so brainless that you were just giving for no reason, GET REAL!

The truth is we thought we were investing in having a future with you and we gave because we loved and cared, don't cheapen it and don't try to make us look crazy after you have accepted everything, let's just be real, fair, and truthful about the matter!

I wish we all had the ability to see into the future to know if we should deal with this person or not, but life has to be lived and we don't have the luxury of knowing how things will turn out before we get involved.

We do, however, have clues, sign posts and signals that if we chose to see will alert us to D R A M A, before we are in it.

God has given us His word as a Guidebook for our lives.

HIT BY A TON OF BRICKS!

WOMEN, I FEEL YOUR PAIN!

I can sincerely and honestly say that I experienced what you are going to feel when your relationship is over.

It will feel just like a ton of bricks hit you, because we have built our world around the hope of having a future with this man.

I felt so helpless, exhausted, frustrated and in utter shock when he said he did not love me, I resembled a deflated balloon.

I think that I went for so long without anyone in my life and I had waited so long to have a man that my hurt was intensified.

To me it felt like someone had died and no one was in mourning but me.

My life had to be altered now because I had built my world around him. I had to re-think my actions and go on with my future without him.

I knew I was going to have to start rebuilding my financial situation and repair my credit, but who was going to help me repair my broken heart?

This is where God stepped in for me, for three reasons, because He Sees, He Knows and He cares.

He Sees.

Nothing we ever do will take God by surprise.

He knew my desperate search for love would lead me down this forbidden path and He knew that I would have to pay the consequences of my decision.

He Knows.

Since God is All Knowing, He knew what I was going to get myself into, but most importantly of all, He knew as a result of my actions, I would desperately need Him to rescue me.

God feels our pain and cries with us and He knew just how broken hearted I would be.

He Cares.

I matter to God—He is a concerned and loving Father, with a sincere and genuine interest in every aspect of my life and He desires to guide me with his infinite wisdom, If I only ask him.

God has allowed me through His care and loving kindness to come into the knowledge that no one can guarantee that any of us will never be hurt in our lives, but with his love and guidance, we can avoid dangerous pitfalls in the future.

He has shown me how to search within myself for the answers, to retrace my steps and carefully examine my actions that led to this situation and to devote some "ME" time for myself for me to learn just who I am and love myself.

I am so grateful to know that this Great and Wonderful God takes the time to be concerned about me, I have made a conscious decision to let God wrap me in His loving arms and let Him hold me until He loves all of my hurt away.

WHY DIDN'T I SEE THIS COMING?

Y*ou can't see your situation, while you are in it!*

RELATIONSHIP STATES

STATE ONE—THE BLINDNESS ZONE

Beware of the "Blindness Zone!"
In this Stage, you are so caught up in infatuation and your eyes are blinded with his handsomeness and your head is in the clouds, it really does have an affect on how you think!

You literally take temporary leave of your senses and lose all sense of reason and your good common sense.

All rational thinking and reasoning are completely shot and we are gone.

We become so caught up, it is as if we really see little hearts over our eyes and for that moment, we are so helpless and weak, we begin to think and say things like, "Sho' is a shame for a man to be so fine," and Have Mercy!

STAGE TWO—THE AWAKENING

This is an awareness Stage.
All infatuation and bliss has worn off at this point and you begin

to see a person's little faults, conduct, attitudes, behavior and character traits that were hidden from you in the beginning, but they were there, but they are now beginning to surface.

It is so funny that it has been said that when two people meet for the first time, they are not really meeting each other, but representatives of each other.

So you begin to see the real "Them" and secrets creep up and hidden drama is revealed, but at this point, you have developed intense feelings for this person and you say to yourself, "Well, It really isn't that bad and you feel that you can live with whatever it is, or you will attempt to change them.

Once a person gets comfortable and starts letting their hair down, as a matter of speaking, their "True Self" comes out.

The only thing that can come out of you, is what is in you!

STAGE THREE—LET IT ALL HANG OUT!

The Thrill Is Gone!
The excitement and the thrill is all the way gone at this point and you begin to say "Just What Did I Ever See In This Person In The First Place?"

You begin to resent this person and you discover the harsh reality that this relationship is not for me.

This stage is the most horrific and devastating because we can really see the light and all of the masks are removed.

It is in this Stage that the D R A M A, really begins, because we have probably paid out untold sums of monies, purchased things, added them to our lease, live together, made investments in furniture, share banking accounts, purchased cell phones, assisted in purchasing cars, helped pay child support, bailed them out of jail, and even had one or more babies for our men.

It is as if you are married, but with no documentation and now you are splitting up and it feels like you are getting a divorce.

The parting of ways is so emotionally draining and now all you want is out.

None of this is what God wants for us.

All of this is too much to endure for someone you have made no *commitment to and no promise of a future live together in anticipation of marriage.*

EMERGENCY! RESCUE! "911"

RESTORATION OF OUR MEN

O ur men need our help. My experience taught me that I am a product of the "New Age Woman."
Women are now assuming so many Non-traditional Roles, making salaries that exceed our men, Progressive, Professional, College Graduates, Heads of Households, Administrators, Heads of Corporations, who are multifaceted and ready to take on the same challenges of any man.

Women's Liberation brought about many rights of women, making us equal to our men and then we began to challenge them. The weaker vessel became the stronger.

I became a **"Sugar Momma"** to my man because of this "Role Reversal" as a result of this present Society.

The higher up the economic ladder we go, the lower it makes our men feel.

Our men are being overwhelmed by being challenged and by being made to look useless, invaluable, nonessential and just plain "unnecessary."

Men feel threatened and that their very manhood is on trial and in question.

Many men have not even had the presence of a father in the home to model after and some don't even know who their father is.

My man never even saw his father; he was the result a very

brief relationship and his father was out of the mother's life long before his birth. As a result of this, he always felt like he was not wanted, confirmed by the fact that his father never even tried to contact with him.

I am not trying to make an excuse for him, but I do believe, "You can't be what you can see."

Your heart has to go out for our men who suffer these types of horrific situations. Yes, a woman can raise a good man, but there is nothing like a real **Father!**

Can you imagine being thrown away like you are a piece of trash to be discarded, as if you don't even matter?

Men have been robbed of their responsibility to feel important, to feel needed, to fell the gratification of providing and taking care of their families.

Women now challenge men in the home, the workplace, and in society as a whole. We also began to kick our men and put them down by saying things like "I am the Breadwinner now," "I make more than you," "I wear the pants now" and "What good are you? I'll do it myself!"

God's established ordained order is now being challenged by the spirit of the Devil. He hates what God has established and he is trying to use us to break our men down.

Results of this breakdown can be seen in the destruction of our families, destroying the family structure, ultimately removing the husband/father and any type of male influence from the home.

The breakdown of a man happens when he continually becomes challenged and he gives up the fight and accepts being taken care of instead of the Caretaker and provider.

He will forfeit his manhood for a life of unemployment, and taking the easy road for pampering, while losing his self-esteem, his very purpose and sense of significance. Feeling very unnecessary.

Men are selling out to being taken care of because we women are so hungry for love and lonely, they don't mind telling you, "I can be bought, if the price is right!"

Our men are suffering from a lack of responsibility and we are the catalyst, the reason, sole cause.

We need to rescue our men by reversing this deadly trend,

because we are helping and aiding in the destruction of his self-image and self-esteem.

I became a person who aided my man by becoming a "Caretaker."

Caretakers are dangerous because they feel needed when they have someone that has to be taken care of.

Caretakers also feel that when they don't have a person in their lives who needs to be fixed or taken care of, that they are useless.

It seems to give them a purpose for being. We all want to matter to someone and this is the way they fulfill this need.

Our men are being victimized by women who need "Needy" people to feel needed.

Sometimes we enable our men to become weak, dependent and in such a state of neediness as a tactic to keep them in our lives.

This is not love, but Control! Who said you could play "Santa Clause?"

This is so sad.

Women, we have reduced our men to a type of "Prostitution" combined with "Slavery."

We make the money, we pay them for doing nothing but keeping us sexually satisfied, and at the same time, we are sort of a "Master" over you by telling you what to do.

We are creating a generation of weak, hopeless, dependent, worthless men, who feel that their performance in the bedroom is their sole contribution to the relationship.

We have created a species of Male, who feel that what is between their legs is the "Great Equalizer," as if this is what makes him a man. I am not hating on you Brothers, I realize that we share the blame for this attitude; I am just keeping it real—OK?

I found out that this is just what I was doing to my man and hurting myself also, I discontinued with this dysfunctional relationship only to send him into the arms and bed of another "Caretaker," who not only moved him in with her, but married him.

My heart was so shocked, I became so overwhelmed at the news that the pressure and stress was too great for me, because I knew what this woman was in for.

I was so devastated, simply because I assumed that surely no *other woman would want him in his wretched condition.*

I cried at first and was in a state of shock, partly because I still loved him, but I had to make a conscious decision whether or not I could continue to watch him go through a vicious cycle that seemed to be a mission of self-destruction and carelessness.

It is different when misfortune happens to find you, it is another thing to go looking for it and to bring unnecessary drama on yourself.

I cried because of all of the effort, ideas, methods, tactics, I used that I thought would help him want to make a change did not effect him, nor bring about any change.

All I did was apply a band-aide to a fatal wound. All of the sex, love and giving of monies, lectures and advice could not bring about change because it was going to have to be brought about by him making a conscious decision, a mental effort upon his part to want to change.

The problems he had were deeper than I realized and I had to throw up the white flag of surrender, not because I did not love or care for him, but my efforts to continue with my "Caretaking" would have only continued to keep the flame of dependency on me smoldering.

When I met him, he was serving time on the weekends for fines and traffic violations and I would later learn that within three weeks of his marriage, he was back in jail again, continuing the cycle.

This is just one case and I am sure there are more, but I know that we have a lot of broken men, who if they had an opportunity to have a good, solid person to give them a helping hand, would pull themselves up from their boot straps and make a change, the only problem is, you can't tell who they are.

God will show you and reveal to you through his spirit who these people are and that they are ready to make a change. God will also let you know that he has called you to assist in restoring the person's life.

Many of us women will have to stand by the sides of men who will be down on their luck and will need a helping hand, but that is all it will be, not to take over their lives and to try to be a "Caretaker" and simply equip them to continue to become dependent upon us without any effort, input, or participation in helping themselves.

We have to be compassionate to know that there are so many pitfalls that our men can get involved in such as Drugs, Jail, for any type of offenses, some of which they have been wrongly accused, some in jail for child support, their finances affected by recent lay-offs, downsizing, divorces that have left them penniless due to paying alimony and leaving the woman with the house and the car, alcoholism, medical illnesses that have rendered them "disabled."

Life brings some type of drama or hardship to all of us, and we as women will have to realize that we may just meet some of these men, who may have had this in their past, but they have changed and God is saving many such men like these.

We as women need to be very careful how we look down our noses at our men, just because we are in high profile positions, with our corporate suits on, because we are not all what we seem either.

I am not saying that you need to lower your standards, but I have learned that many of us have unrealistic expectations of our men.

A man can be a good man with an average, blue collar job, just as long as he is responsible and making an honest living from being a janitor, security guard, heck to even bringing home a steady check from a fast food restaurant, at least he is responsible to do the best he can!

Sometimes our expectations are set so high that we can't find anybody to fit our checklist of what we want and it is because the checklist is flawed. There is no perfect man, and incidentally, you probably aren't the perfect woman!

I am not saying you should go out and pick up any "Joe" off the street and move him in with you and you start taking care of him, NO!

As women, we need to slow our row anyway. We are so desperate and lonely that we are quick to move to fast in relationships, get to know a man first and learn about him before you sleep with him and move him in, and giving him full access to your car and to everything you hold near and dear.

It is very confusing to men, some of us want to be their "Sugar Momma" and take care of them, and some of us want to be "Gold Diggers, by taking a man to the cleaners by having him pay for our hair, nails, pay our rent, bills and then we don't even like him.

We have to remember that our men, if they are responsible men, need to pay their own rent, car note, bills and living expenses for themselves. Our present times are hard, too hard for a person to take care of all of your needs and maintain his own needs as well.

It is equally wrong women to use a man only for what he can give to you, and for us to size him up by the car he drives, never even expecting to have a future with him.

We women can be ruthless, heartless and "cold blooded" sometimes only using a man for what we can get out of him and have reduced him to being treated like a piece of meat, or a sexual toy—Men have feelings too!

It tears me up inside to see a sweet, decent, hardworking, sincere man being played like a "Fiddle," because he is so taken with a woman's physical appearance, that he becomes blinded and used just like a dish rag and hung out to dry.

I know there are a lot of good, hardworking men, some who will even work two and three jobs to make sure that their families are fed and that they are contributing, and heading their homes.

Some single men work several jobs to try and buy the love of a woman, You can't buy love.

If a woman is only interested in your money and what kind of a car you drive, completely ignoring your character, personality, and intellect, it will make you feel a sense of emptiness and loss because you are not being fairly judged for who you are, but for what you have to offer.

If you start your relationship based on the material, this goes for men and women, you must keep up this image and it will probably require that you do even more to maintain it.

THE TRUTH OF THE WHOLE MATTER AND THE BOTTOM LINE!!

In my desperate search for love, I discovered that men and women each have our faults, but my story developed out of seeing what I did as a woman to contribute to the problem rather than helping it.

The truth of the matter is that we are equally wrong—*women for trying to take care of men and for men accepting that kind of life with no intent to participate in assisting in your own well-being.*

We need to realize that God has established a divine order and that we have struck out on our own ways and abandoned what he has ordained for our lives, both men and women.

God wants to restore order in our lives and put this thing back into perspective to help us all get what is best for us.

We all have the same genuine need and that is that we all want to be loved, respected and appreciated. We all want to find the right partner or mate that God has ordained for us.

Men and Women are at war with one another and we are destroying all types of relationships because we are at odds with each other.

We need to hurry up and discover that we are fighting the wrong enemy! We are in a drastic state of confusion, and where there is confusion, there is the Devil, trying to tear down and destroy the perfect Will of God.

I am not trying to say that we women are the total blame, but much of it weighs upon us. I believe that men will only do to us what we allow them to do.

I believe that with God, no situation is hopeless and that we can turn this thing around, if we stick together, pray and seek God's face and entreat him to help us to become strong backbones of our homes and our communities once again, with His help, we can begin to restore order and to bring our men back to their rightful place, right by our sides.

God never intended for men or women to date all of our lives, He intended for you to marry and build your life with a lifelong mate.

God never intended for you to create such a thing as a "Sex Life." Just continuing to sleep around from partner to partner with no intent of making a commitment to marriage.

God does not want us to be in and out of relationships that tear our hearts apart, and scar you so badly that you don't even feel like being in a relationship, so hurt, so many times that you even begin to feel that maybe you aren't even worth loving.

Women, we began to let our standards down, with sexual revolutions and this new age doctrine. We got real confused and began treating our boyfriends as if they were our husbands.

Opening up our hearts, wallets, emotions and our legs, to give them everything that is precious to us, then move them in giving them access to everything, as if we went through the marriage ceremony and we have a marriage certificate and wedding ring.

Some of us try to perpetrate and call him our Fiancé', but somehow the marriage never seems to take place even after several babies are born to the so-called union.

We need to check ourselves in a hurry, so that the sooner we put ourselves in check our men will take their proper place as well.

We need to rescue our men by reversing this deadly trend.

We are crippling our men, by taking care of them and we are hindering the Will of God.

God has given man a "Purpose," which means the original intent, The Will of God or the Original Intent of God.

God's original intent for our men is for them to be the bread-

winner, the head of the household, the protector, the provider to be responsible and a defender of all that belongs to him.

*In this present age men have been stripped and displaced of their original position and purpose intended by God and they wander around aimlessly in confusion because they do not have a clear self-image and direction, he is in an "**Identity Crisis**."*

*Many men are confused even about what it means to be a "**Man**."*

Every God created being has a God intended purpose for being.

Man's purpose is constantly being challenged in this present era.

Anytime, something is not being used for its original purpose, then you have total misuse and abuse.

I saw this point clearly looking back over my relationship. I am so overwhelmed over the damage that I helped cause in my man's life in the name of "HELP."

I caused him to get his signals crossed over his purpose and to become weaker each time I did for him, I robbed him of his right to do for himself.

Helping is really a form of hurting! You wouldn't give a pair of crutches to a man who is able to walk, would you?

Helping someone who can do for themselves is crippling and as long as you are going to do it, Why should he?

We must begin to restore proper order, Divine Order to perform and function.

Our men are our most valuable asset and in our civilization they are a threatened species. Our men are our foundation.

Let us unite and help men to be men again.

Our men, who are our Kings need to be restored to their rightful inheritance and re-claim their God given Thrones.

We cannot do this on our own, but as we pray and ask God's guidance and direction, He will teach us as we take a stand and act like the Queens God made us to be, we will take control of the reigns and once again live by Godly morals, values and principles and with time, faith and patience, we will all regain our ordained original purpose.

BURY THE PAST AND MOVE FORWARD

<u>LEARN FROM YOUR MISTAKE</u>

*No one can move forward while looking back!!!
We must let the past be just that THE PAST!*
We cannot change it, it happened, but we can make some positive changes for the future.

Let no bitterness or hatred linger in your heart for the person you feel wronged or took advantage of you, especially if you were a contributor to that experience.

Many of us women are in messes that we created all on our own. No one held a gun to our heads and forced us to give up our money, time, hearts, feelings, emotions and love.

God will deliver us out of a lot of situations that were not His Will for us, but because we have the power of **Choice and Decision**, *we don't always use them in our own best interest.*

Don't beat yourself up to bad for what happened, just see the truth and get free.

We all want to be loved and accepted, but we must realize that Love is a Choice.

If someone does not choose to love you, there is nothing you can do, all the money, sex, presents or gifts, favors, giving of time, listening and being there for them, meeting their every need completely, putting your life on hold, setting aside all of your dreams and goals, putting your desires on the back burner, for the sake of pleasing another person, **JUST DOES NOT WORK!**

Unless another chooses and decides to love you, you can't make them!

People give us signs by what they say and do and even better what they don't say or do.

Don't be in denial and overlook the obvious.

My man was not in love with me and he gave me signs, not wanting to be near me, leaving the bedroom to go sleep on the couch, not wanting to spend quality time with me.

When you find that you have nothing to talk about when the television is off, when you can be with him, but you still feel isolated and all alone because there is nothing to say or you are talking but they are pre-occupied and not hearing a word you say.

Look with your eyes and not with your heart, don't deny the truth no matter how much it hurts, and then decide within yourself, I deserve better than this.

I came to this conclusion and I turned the microscope on myself to determine what sort of emotional deficiency, loneliness, void and emptiness, drove me to this state, so that I can identify what went wrong in my life, so that this misguided behavior will never be repeated.

The answer all boils down to loving God and then loving yourself.

Once you see how much God loves you, you begin to see your value and wholeness through His eyes and you begin to take on a new attitude because of what He thinks of you.

When you begin to view life and relationships with this new attitude you begin to ask questions that will protect you from relationship disasters such as the following such as:

Do you love yourself first before seeking love from another?
Do you know what real love is?
Does this person really love you?
Are you dating with the purpose of marrying or just for sex?
Is this the person the Lord has selected for you?

Do you know the difference between love and sex?
What do you expect this person to bring to the relationship?
Does this person believe in God?
Does this person have any goals, or future aspirations?
Do they have a bank account, pay taxes, or vote?
Are they in any other committed relationship or marriage?
Are they Drug free, free of sexual disease or aids?
Are there any criminal offenses that will affect time with you?
Are you getting the love you are giving in return?
Are they considerate and concerned about you?
Are they in control of their emotions or fly off the handle?
Do they have a calm and understanding heart?
Do they strive to protect you and your feelings from harm?
Do they have a respect for all women and his mother?
What is their attitude toward finances, do they pay bills or Obligations, or are they wasteful and careless?
Do they have good moral values and respect for the law?
Does this person exhibit a genuine concern for you as a Person or is it all about "Them?"
Does this person offer advice out of concern for your well being?

Make sure that each of you communicates what you expect.
(You may say, how am I going to find out all of this, by talking and communicating with one another. Many of us move too fast and may already be sleeping with someone without knowing the answers to these and more questions).

VALENTINE'S DAY

It is Valentine's Day, February 14, 2002. Well, Here it is again! After what I've been through you'd think I'd have a Valentine by now!

This is a day of Love. It means flowers, candy, cards and extravagant dinners, diamonds, jewelry, champagne, etc.

Today, for me is a symbol of a pure and true Love, given to me from God, because God has freed me from my six years of bondage and an end to a form of slavery that I inflicted upon myself.

I am completely and utterly fulfilled, no longer feeling like I am incomplete, unfulfilled, unworthy or unloved because I don't have a man in my life at the present time.

I am now happy because God loved me first and His love has filled all of the empty places in my life and restored my self-esteem, self-pride and dignity as a woman.

Today, for me represents my liberation and a soul celebration to signify that I am made whole, no longer inadequate because I measure who I am or what I am or whether I am happy because I do or don't have a man.

God has shown me how much He loves me and what He thinks of me and to be at peace with myself and love myself, because He already does and not to place so much emphasis on this as a fact of validation.

Seeing myself through God's eyes, showed me how precious and valuable I am to Him and the awesome price God paid by sacrificing Jesus Christ to die on the cross in my place was a major turning point in my life.

Jesus is the Best Thing that ever happened in my life. The day I said, Yes, to the Lord and asked Him to come into my heart and fill me with the light of His Love is more powerful than any imaginable force on this earth and it healed me and set me free.

For those of you who are in a desperate search for real love, I dare you to give this a try, It is sooo much, I can't contain it all in my heart, it is so phanthumless and infinite.

Thank you God, for revealing yourself to me and sharing your love with me. God's love came deep inside my heart and totally transformed me to the point that I now want only the best for myself, just as He wants the best for me.

I came through a very hard and self-imposed lesson, but God brought me out and I feel like a totally different woman and I want to share all of this with you—So rejoice with me, because guess what, God is going to do the same thing for you through this book and through His Love.

I can see all of us former Sisters of Bondage as we graduate, while the angels in heaven are playing "Pomp and Circumstance on their harps in heaven and we walk in true freedom and liberation, loving ourselves and loving our God.

THE "GREATEST NEWS" YOU WILL EVER HEAR!

GOD IS REAL, GOD IS ALIVE, AND HE LOVES YOU!

*T*his is the greatest news you will ever hear in your lifetime, and that is **GOD LOVES YOU!**
You can take this personal, because it is meant for you to know it as an individual.

God knows who you are, He is absolutely aware of everything that concerns you. I know it is remarkable to believe, but it is true. He knows everything about you and He is concerned about every area of your life.

God is aware of all of your faults, problems, hurts, attitudes and every personality trait you possess.

It is true that God Loves You and there is nothing you can do about it, because it is not based on you, but on Him and it was His choice to love us first, just because He wanted to. God is the Master Creator and you have been made in His image with tender loving care, simply for the purpose of loving you through fellowship with Him. To have a friendship with you.

God's nature is Love and if we are to ever discover what true love really is, we need to turn our hearts to Him and establish a relationship with Him and make Him our "First Love" and give Him first place in our lives.

God's love is for the taking and the most wonderful thing is that you didn't have to earn it. It is almost too good to be true, but it is.

In a day like today, when there is so much hatred, evil, animosity and strife, the world is so cold and people treat you so bad, sometimes you are hurt so bad that you feel like dying!

God knew our hearts would suffer hurts, devastation and pain so intense, and unbearable, God knew that this day would be one of the worst eras the world has ever known, where people are so cold and heartless, He knew we would only be able to survive by knowing that His love will sustain us. He knew we could face anything, as long as we knew He would be with us.

Never before in the history of the world have relationships and marriages been in such jeopardy. Men and women are so badly brokenhearted and damaged.

God never intended for us to be a generation of hurting people, walking around with fatal and and deep gaping wounds.

Many of us are carrying childhood scars, bruises and past hurts that have been so devastating we can't tell anyone, and yet, we go on from day to day as if nothing ever happened, but deep in our hearts we cannot escape such experiences of rape, molestation, physical, mental and emotional abuses.

Sometimes you hurt so badly and feel so alone and unloved that you feel that nobody loves you, then you begin to feel worthless, invaluable and insignificant, even to the point that you feel that you don't even matter to anyone.

You cry yourself to sleep at night, only to wake up to another day of the same emptiness and void of the previous day. Going to jobs we hate and following the same dead routine feeling unfulfilled.

God knows that all of the things we went through and the scars we bare may have been caused by evil people that were in our lives that made a conscious decision to hurt us, God did not cause this, people do evil of their own will, not his.

Many evil people did these heinous actions while many were young, innocent, trusting and unable to protect themselves.

No matter how bad the past or what happened, God's love can heal you and make you brand new again.

All of us yearn to be loved, accepted and feel that we belong.

The "Greatest News" You Will Ever Hear!

We are all in search of answers to such questions as:
"Why was I born?"
"What is my purpose?"
"Where do I fit in and Just where is my place in this world?"
God says in response to these questions, "In all thy ways acknowledge Him, and He shall direct they path."
In seeking God, He will reveal the answers to these questions.
We all want to give love and be loved in return, but loving God will make you whole and enable you to love yourself and others.
God made each of us with an innate desire for fellowship and a yearning that only He can fill.
We often pour our love into everything else but God and this need never gets filled and becomes misdirected to the wrong things or the wrong people.
God made us for fellowship and friendship with Him and since God is Love, the measuring stick begins with Him.
No one knows you better than God who made you, Trust Him to determine and define what true love really is.
*All you have to do is accept God's love for you demonstrated through the greatest act of Love ever shown in the world, **John 3:16:***
"For God so loved the world that He gave His only begotten Son, that whosoever believeth on Him will not perish, but will have everlasting life."
I count the Love of God as the greatest gift I could have ever discovered in my lifetime and it is the single most important event that has happened to me in my life.
Knowing that God Loves me has been the pinnacle point and the zenith of my life.
Knowing God loves me, takes me through every trial and adversity I have encountered. Knowing that He cares about me and that He is real, suddenly makes my load easier to bear.
God wrapped Himself in sinful flesh in the person of Jesus Christ and because He loved me so much, He came down to look for me and to reclaim me as His child, as one of His lost sheep that he needed to recover.
My recovery and redemption cost Jesus His life and He died in my place, for my sins and for yours, Jesus the sweet Lamb of God,

had made me righteous and bridged the gap of my lost soul back to the heart of God.

My life has worth since Jesus died for me; I have a plan and a destiny to love Him in return.

This same unconditional love is yours also and it is a steadfast love that will never fade away, no matter what!

Simply reach for the Hem of His garment as He passes by and that touch and point of contact will surely make you whole.

You will find rest for your soul, and God will show you that everything will be alright.

Give your worries, burdens, impossibilities and your messed up life to Him and let Him show you His Divine purpose and plan for your life.

Every life is valuable and priceless to God, and you really matter to Him.

*Stop throwing your life away and say **"Yes"** to God and accept the gift of Jesus Christ and His finished works performed for you and watch Him make SOMETHING BEAUTIFUL OF YOUR LIFE!*

TO RECEIVE THIS GREAT GIFT FOR YOU

YOU HAVE ONLY TO ACCEPT IT!

You must recognize and accept the precious gift of God in the person of Jesus Christ, who died for us, when we were lost and in lost and in our sins.

Recognize your need for God in your life, sincerely repent of your sins and accept Jesus Christ to be the Savior of your soul, who became the Sacrificial Lamb, who went to the Cross and died to redeem you.

Jesus literally took our place to restore a broken fellowship with God by standing in the gap for us. There are a lot of things we can try on our own to be free from sin, but the question and answer is, "What can wash away my sins?, "Nothing, but the blood of Jesus!"

Since there was no one else who was worthy of such a task, God came down in the form of human flesh in the person of Jesus to do this Himself for us.

The greatest demonstration of Love, since the creation of the universe was shown in this act.

"Greater Love hath no man than this, Herein is true love, pure, deep and everlasting.

LOVE, is the most powerful force on earth there is!!

This is where your participation is critical and necessary.

You see, even though God knows you need him, it is your choice whether or not to accept His gift. You were born with a "Free Will"

*God will not force Himself upon you, you must **invite Him in**, He will never refuse anyone's invitation.*

The power of God's Love is shown to us once again, because God could force Himself on us and make us all like robots, being forced to love Him in return, whether He wanted to or not, but you know and I know that when we want someone to love us, we want it to be because they made the conscious choice to do so, because they wanted to.

When we make this decision on our own, then God knows that we did it because we wanted to, not because we were tricked, coerced or forced, then He knows when we freely offer up our hearts to Him, that it is genuine.

There is so much joy in my life now, because God showed me my worth and value to Him, and that He took the time to let me take an analytical look at myself as He showed me to Love and Respect myself was the way out,

Since Jesus paid the price for my freedom, why should I remain in bondage? There is no reason to and anyone else who wants to be free can too.

Jesus desires to do the same thing for you, man or woman. He wants to give your life a brand new start and we can all use a second chance!

The Sacrificial Lamb of God desires to cleanse your life through His blood too.

I realize that God was merciful to me and that I could have died while I was in my messy situation, and I could still be a slave to trying to buy a man's love and force him to love me, but I am free of that.

Make a decision right now to open your heart to God, because none of us knows where death may be for us, and that tomorrow is not promised to us.

Accept Jesus as your Personal Savior, while the blood yet runs warm in your veins, while you have time and let God love you with a true, pure and everlasting love, in the way the you were meant to be loved.

It is not normal for a person to refuse a "Gift," especially when it is free and it didn't cost you anything. What do you say?, You *have nothing to lose, but everything to gain!*

God is real, loving, understanding, caring and good and He went to an awful lot of trouble to prove His love to you.

God wants to shower us with blessings and goodness and he wants to act in our behalf and fight our battles and handle our problems.

God created us to Love us. It is so good, it is hard to understand, but how I come to understand God, is not nearly as precious as knowing that God already understands You and Me!

Don't try to analyze, just receive it and **Thank God for His LOVE!**

SCRIPTURAL PROOF OF HOW GOD FEELS ABOUT YOU!

JEREMIAH 31:3
The Lord hath appeared of old unto us, saying, Yea, I have loved thee with an everlasting love, therefore with lovingkindness have I drawn thee.

JOHN 3:16
For God so loved the world, that He gave His only begotten Son, that whosoever believeth in Him should not perish, but have everlasting life.

1 JOHN 4:19
We love Him, because He first loved us.

PROVERBS 8:17
I love them that love me; and those that seek me early shall find me.

1 JOHN 3:16
Hereby perceive we the Love of God, because He laid down His life for us.

SAINT JOHN 15:13
Greater love hath no man than this, that a man lay down His life for his friends.

JOHN 16:27
For the Father Himself loveth you . . . . .

1 JOHN 4:8
God is Love.

ROMANS 8:38—39 *(What can separate us from the Love of God?)*
For I am persuaded, that neither death, nor life, nor angels, nor principalities, nor powers, nor things present, nor things to come, nor height, nor depth nor any other creature, shall be able to separate us from the love of God, which is in Christ Jesus our Lord.

ROMANS 5:8, 9, 10 AND 13
But God commendeth His love toward us, in that, while we were yet sinners, Christ died for us.

Much more then, being now justified by His blood, we shall be saved from wrath through Him.

For if, when we were enemies, we were reconciled to God by the death of His Son, much more, being reconciled, we shall be saved by His life.

For whosoever shall call upon the name of the Lord shall be saved.

So if you are not saved, ask God to save you so that you can begin to really live a life of "Real Love" and like me you can end your "Desperate Search for Love"